Olivia Brown

The Affair

A Journal Series

PUBLISH AMERICA

PublishAmerica
Baltimore

First printing

You can visit the author at
www.OliviaBrownBooks.com

ISBN: 1-59286-570-4
PUBLISHED BY PUBLISHAMERICA, LLLP
www.publishamerica.com
Baltimore

Printed in the United States of America

Dedication

For My Husband—My Inspiration, My Love

Acknowledgements
& Special Thanks to:

Sandra, Mother & Friend
Robin, Sister & Supporter
Christine Maniaci, Family Friend
Sarah Maniaci of Piaci Imaging

Table of Contents

Chapter 1

The Journal—Part One

Dear Journal,

"You're a hopeless romantic!" he tells me.

Well, he was right. My husband knows me inside and out. But being a hopeless romantic isn't necessarily the best thing to be. I grew up watching soap operas and dreaming of a romance like that of star-crossed lovers. I guess most girls do, but they grow out of it, right? I thought so, but I wasn't one of them. Growing up doesn't make it easier to handle reality. Often, it makes it impossible. The older you get, the harder it becomes to face the truth about life or yourself.

I am** a hopeless romantic. I still yearn to be touched as if I were a porcelain doll. I still want to be kissed tenderly and slowly. I suppose those feelings led to **the affair.

I've been happily married for almost six years, even though I've known my husband for about ten years. We've experienced many hard times, changing and growing throughout it all. It's those changes that made me want more. When you first fall in love with someone, you can't imagine there will ever be anyone else to take his place. After many years, you begin to realize that someone has taken his place and you don't recognize the person you've married. It starts gradually, noticing one day that your husband doesn't look at you the same as he did when you two began. Then another day you notice that you don't look at him the same either. Eventually, you notice you don't see what you want to see in each other. Consequently, it's up to you both to decide how to handle the realization that your love for each other has changed.

Upon discovering those feelings, I didn't handle it well. My husband and I were drifting apart. Our marriage had become strained due to several external influences, as well as some internal ones. It seemed as though our relationship was constantly weathering some type of storm. There were so many disappointments eroding our resolve and our power. For instance, we learned that both of our families' love was conditional and we couldn't count on them for anything. From the very beginning, we knew it was just "us" against the world. Who knew the world was so damned powerful? I didn't.

Battle after battle, we struggled—credit card debt, unemployment, medical bills, car repairs, you name it and it happened to us. We even managed to stay together despite my husband's brief infidelity. His heartfelt plea for forgiveness was one I couldn't reject. I knew he loved me by the tears in his eyes and the tremble in his voice. He knew I could have left, but he confessed anyway; I was oblivious otherwise. I never had to know and he knew that too. So I knew I couldn't leave him for that. After everything, I didn't want to leave him for anything. When our marriage finally seemed to be healing from the betrayal, I didn't realize how scarred I really was. I just wanted it all to go away. I felt denied of romance, passion, and ecstasy, but mostly, I felt empty, cold and scared. I have to admit, though, I was proud of our integrity and our endurance. We continued to combat each problem with all that we had. I guess when the dust settled, there wasn't much left. That's when I began accepting visits from him.

I met him around the time I met my husband. Although I loved my husband, the love for this man was one of madness and passion. I was intoxicated by his very existence, fighting the hard fight to make him mine. Ever since I was a teenager, I longed to be his. Now after all of these years, the past collided with the present. When the connection between my husband and I began to change, I didn't expect to be thrown into this emotional hurricane. But, there I was, thinking of a man that was not my husband. I could no longer deny that I still wanted to fall in love and be in love with the same intensity as the very first moment I saw him....

Chapter 2

The First Moment

It was the summer of 1991. I was bike riding, as I often did during my vacation. I had been all over the neighborhood several times, but I couldn't remember ever going down that street before.

As I rode by, I looked to my right and there he was—a specimen of pure beauty. I'd never seen a guy in real life that looked as if he were carved from a slab of marble. As he stood on the front lawn, involved in a conversation with one of the local boys, I was able to take a mental photograph. He had skin of gold and hair of dark satin, which was pulled into a ponytail on top and cut low on the sides. He was wearing a black tank top with black pants and no shoes. ***You should have seen him.*** His back was pure muscle with wings (side and oblique muscles) that made him look as though he could take flight. His face was unusual to me. I couldn't tell what nationality he was because he was ***so unique***. In fact, he was the most unusual guy I'd ever seen—exotic and rare—probably on the endangered species list. ***I was immediately captivated.***

As quickly as I was being pulled into a black hole of infatuation was as quickly as I heard a voice scream, {"LOOK OUT!"} I was so busy looking at him, while still pedaling, that I was almost completely humiliated. There's something to be said about that little voice in one's head. If it hadn't been for that voice, I would have surely pedaled myself into a parked car. To this day, I believe that if I had actually hit that car, I would have crawled under my house and taken up residence as a troll.

After narrowly escaping such an extreme disaster, I realized that girls like me don't have guys like him. Girls like me only dream of guys like him and I was already an expert at dreaming!

I'll never even get close to him, I thought, after hurrying to the next block. *I'll never even see him again. So, I should just be glad that I didn't splatter on that windshield like a misguided mosquito. Life goes on*, I mused.

I started to be overjoyed at the thought that, at the very least, I was able to see someone—with my very own eyes—so wonderfully made. I knew that girls like me could look, but could never touch. Or could we?

Chapter 3

Back to School

In all honesty, I hadn't thought much of him after that day. I had made peace with the fact that I'd never see him again. Although I was almost positive that the house he had been standing in front of was his, I couldn't just show up on his doorstep. I didn't know how old he was. I didn't know if he had a girlfriend. I didn't even know his name. However, if there were a million things that I didn't know about him, there was one thing I was sure of: ***He'd never fall for me!***

School was starting and I had been enrolled in an art class. I still remember trying to drop that course. I hadn't signed up for it and I didn't know anything about art. I wasn't interested in that class at all—until the very first day. Everything changed when I walked into the room.

I can't believe it! It's him! Oh my God, I wasn't dreaming! He's real and he's right in front of me! I was screaming inside.

That's when that little voice took over. {"Get real. He'll never even notice your existence."}

Why would he? I was an over-achieving tenth grader working towards a scholarship to Michigan State University. I was always known for being a brainy teacher's pet and not much more. What did I have in common with him anyway? I discovered that the mystery man was an artist. I didn't know anything about art and I could barely draw. I found out later that I was put in that class to develop a "well-rounded" personality by participating in a variety of curriculums. Most importantly, though, I realized that ***he was out of my league!***

A few weeks go by and all I can do is stare. The beauty of the stare is the daydream that develops.

I'm crazy to think that he'd ever notice me.

Maybe I'd be crazier not to at least try. Either way, I was losing my mind and myself in his eyes.

The voice chimed in again. {"You are more than crazy if you think that anything you do would be of interest to him. Not only hasn't he given you the time of day, but the scowl that he slings your way seems to tell you everything you need to know."}

Stupid voice. It had a point though. Every glance stolen from him was one of contempt.

But why? Am I that repulsive? Are my glasses a sure giveaway of my inadequacy?

I tried to forget. Every time I saw him, in class, in the hallways or in front of school, my heart pounded so loudly that I knew someone else could hear it.

{"HELLO!"} There's that voice again. {"He's a bad boy. Come on, you're a good girl—for the most part. He probably has a million girls falling at his feet. **If** he were interested, you'd just be another notch in his belt, another worshipper of the ground he walks on, another groupie following his every move. **Get real!**"}

Again with that voice! Again it was right.

He was misunderstood. He skipped school. He was a loner. He was a fighter, a student of Chinese Boxing. He was an untouchable—definitely a bad boy. Whether I liked it or not though, women are attracted to bad boys. I mean, that cliché about nice guys finishing last isn't the problem; it's just that too many times, nice guys don't finish at all.

Okay, so maybe I'm not just an over-achieving book worm. I might need a challenge like this.

{"You'll be sorry,"} whispered that voice.

I thought to myself, *I'm already sorry.*

My childhood wasn't great. After my mom left my psycho, abusive father for the last time, it was just us, her and me. My older brother was a drifter, never really settling down anywhere. He lived with various women but never had a home to call his own. My older sister was in college in the south. Then there was me, the last of the three. I was alone with my cat most of the time because my mom worked a lot. After school I was alone—alone to watch television, to do homework, to clean and yes, let's not forget, to dream. To dream I was someone else, somewhere else, doing something else with someone special. I was only a teenager, but I knew that there was more to me than what everyone saw or expected. Maybe I could get his attention. Maybe I could get him to see what I suspected was inside of me. Maybe I could blossom. Maybe I could try.

Why not? What did I have to lose?

I was already a wallflower with one best friend and two associates. I was already viewed as a shy girl with no wild side. He'd never see me coming. I'd shock everyone—including myself. If I failed, it would be a crushing blow to what little self-esteem I had. But, if I succeeded, I could live the romance of my dreams. I just knew it. I could take the risk. ***He** was worth it.*

Chapter 4

The Plan

After several weeks, I had accomplished a great deal. This was a delicate situation that needed to be handled just right. And, of course, I was clueless as to how I was actually going to pull this off. So I did some investigating first, watching him daily during art class, which allotted me quite a bit of information. The most important discovery was his name—Manùel (man-well) Nelson. Actually, everyone pretty much addressed him as "Manny." I found out his full name later, while *assisting* the art teacher. Honestly, that was just a ploy to get my hands on the attendance cards. *(You know, cards with every student's full name, address and telephone number printed on them.)* Those little cards gave me the upper hand.

As I mentioned earlier, I had been watching Manny daily, or should I say whenever he was in class. I listened to him speak. I watched him draw. I observed his interactions with others. I felt his energy. I fell in love. I know a person could easily say that I was experiencing a "crush" or "puppy love," but I knew it was more. I could confidently assert this as a fact because I was up against some heavy resistance, and I still felt strongly about him.

Not much had changed since the beginning of the school year. He still looked at me as if I was his enemy and I could never get him to speak to me in plain English. It's not that he didn't speak English. Although his mother was of Mexican descent and his father was 75% Irish and 25% Indian, he spoke English eloquently. In fact, he was the most articulate young man I had ever heard speak—but when addressing me, he used riddles. Or he would talk to other people while looking directly at me. It was as if Manny was communicating with me on some subliminal frequency that only I could hear.

It was my "Sweet 16." I remember bringing in a big birthday card for everyone to sign. Actually, it wasn't proper etiquette to supply this myself, but who else was going to do it? Plus it was a great way to get a couple of bucks and a few hundred signatures—the most important signature being Manny's. I was a bit shocked that he even wanted to sign the thing, but he did. In fact, he wrote a birthday message to me—backwards! I couldn't really make it out, so I took the card to the girls' bathroom to decode the message in the mirror. It read, "I hope you get some sex for your birthday, Manny." I realized, at that moment, that there was much more going on between us than I originally thought.

{"Don't read too much into that little note."} That voice was making a return appearance. {"It probably means that he wants to do to you what he does to every other girl who likes him—Love 'em and Leave 'em."}

So far that voice hadn't been wrong, but there's a first time for everything. I became even more determined and decided to make my move. I had a feeling that if I could just have some time alone with him, I could find out what—if anything—was going on between us. I figured that if I could muster up enough courage, maybe I could even reveal my feelings. But where, when, and how? I didn't know much about Manny and I wasn't sure how or where I could actually arrange for us to be alone together. I knew his phone number, but I needed to discuss this with him in person. I couldn't just invite him over—he hardly knew me and I didn't think he'd actually show up. I knew where he lived thanks to the mental picture of him previously taken while he stood in front of his house. So, although I had the address, I didn't need it. That's where I had to go.

I remember leaving school the next day, catching the bus home and walking to my house. All the while trying to talk myself out of going to see Manny.

{"You're crazy. Brave, but crazy!"}

Oh shut up, you! A girl has to do what a girl has to do. I was tired of that voice contradicting me all of the time, although that's the job of your conscience, isn't it? It didn't matter. I wasn't going to let that voice talk me out of doing what I knew I had to do.

I passed by my house. I knew that my mother was at work and wouldn't be home for a couple of hours. I also knew that there was a good chance Manny was at home, since he didn't show up for art class and I hadn't seen him all day.

I continued walking. I walked to the end of my block and made a left turn. Manny's street was about three or four blocks down, but it seemed like the longest walk of my life. I agonized over my decision to show up on his doorstep.

{"You're going to get hurt,"} "You know who" kept saying.

Too late, I was already aching inside. I had to be near him. I just kept thinking of how he would look at me. At first, I thought that he only felt contempt for me, but things gradually changed. I could see Manny's eyes soften towards me when he would look up and realize I had been staring. I felt this intense pull towards him every time he entered the room. Either way, the whole thing was killing me.

Finally, I was in front of the beautiful brick house enclosed with a maroon-colored picket fence. All I had to do now was open the gate and walk up the path to the porch steps.

{"Well, you're here now. I'm even a little curious as to how this will turn out. Go for it!"}

What a time for that voice to be on my side!

I opened the gate slowly and proceeded up the steps. My heart was in my shoes! I walked up the stairs and stood in front of the door.

All I have to do is knock and I'll have my answer, I reasoned.

I was petrified, but I knocked, then I waited.

Well, he's not here, no one's here. So I'll just run screaming away from this house and pretend this whole thing never happened….

I started to turn towards the steps when I heard a noise. I saw the curtain in the door's window move and then the door began to open. It was Manny.

Chapter 5

Over the Threshold

"Hello, Manny. Remember me?" I said while trying to hold back a nervous giggle.

"Of course. I know you from art class. Olivia Brown, right?" he said with a grin.

Actually, he looked quite tickled by my unexpected visit. I wanted to run, but it was too late. I knew that I had to see this through to the end.

"Right, Olivia Brown, that's me." My voice trembled. "Well, are you busy? Do you have company or something?"

"No, come on in." I was being invited into the lion's den.

"I don't know why I'm here," I spoke softly, "but I had to come."

"I know you did." He was so cocky. It drove me crazy.

"What do you mean by that?"

"I see how you look at me in class. You seem very curious about me. I thought that you would do something to get my attention, but I never thought you'd show up on my doorstep."

"Neither did I. I've never done this sort of thing before."

"I didn't think so. You seem so shy; I can't believe you would ever be bold enough to come over to my house like this. You know we're alone, don't you?"

"Well, I trust you." I said it, but I was starting not to believe it.

"Maybe you shouldn't." His voice was calm.

My heart was beating so fast, I thought I was going to faint.

"What are you going to do? Rape me? 'Cause I can scream pretty loud and I know how to kick a man so that he pees blood for a week."

I tried to sound confident.

"Believe me, you won't *want* to fight," he said plainly. Manny was a lot more confident than I was—and he knew it.

I was dying. I didn't know what was going on. Were we just experiencing some teenage sexual tension? If that's all it was, then I didn't want it. I loved him, and sex was a fear, not a welcomed prospect. I figured I'd play along and see where this was going, but I was pretty sure that he didn't want a soulmate, more like a bedfellow.

Manny was true to his previous form. He baited me with riddles and told me that I was in trouble for challenging him. He revealed that he was purposely trying to repel me, but I was too persistent and determined. Manny never admitted the reason for his calculated deterrence, only that I was going to pay for my rebellion. I was feeling uncomfortable and wanted to change the subject. Slowly, the conversation shifted. I still wasn't sure what was going on between us, but I was so energized with adrenaline, I couldn't feel sad or disappointed. ***I felt alive.*** Regardless of what was happening, I was feeling things that I had never experienced before. Good or bad, I didn't want it to end.

"Why weren't you in school today?"

"I was up exercising late last night and I couldn't get up this morning."

I could tell. From the moment I laid eyes on him, I noticed his muscular physique—especially the wings of his back. Once again I had to think to myself, *Truly a beautiful man.*

"Well, um, what are you working on here?" I was making reference to the drawing on the dining table. I hadn't seen that one in class.

Manny sat down at the table and invited me to join him. He told me about the drawing and the plans he had to become a famous artist. After seeing his work, I was sure that he would be a great success. As we talked I began to realize that I had never had a conversation like that with anyone before. It exposed Manny as being the most passionate individual I had ever met. He knew what he wanted and he knew what he liked. As I mentioned before, he spoke very eloquently, especially about things that ignited his spirit, like drawing and martial arts.

Eventually, we went upstairs to Manny's room. I was more relaxed by then and felt that we had developed quite a rapport with each other. I couldn't believe what I saw when I entered. Manny had what one would call an attic bedroom, which he decorated personally. I was awestruck by his creativity. There were crystals hung from every part of his ceiling. There were lights strung from one end of the bedroom to the other, blue lights. I learned later that "blue lights" were Manny's favorite color. His bed was on the floor and it faced a small window that overlooked the street. There was soft music already playing, music that I had never heard before. It was as if he was expecting someone. I desperately wanted to believe *that someone was me*. I hoped that Manny *sensed* my arrival somehow.

After talking to him and seeing that room, I was sure that I wouldn't be able to resist his inevitable seduction. I turned to leave the room, but he stopped me.

"Don't worry. I'm not going to hurt you." He spoke softly, and then smiled.

I really thought that he was referring to emotionally and not physically. I knew I was in over my head. I wondered why I couldn't stop myself. I *needed* to go further.

We walked around the room and ended up sitting on the bed, talking. I found myself watching his lips, which were cherry red and appeared incredibly soft. I had never seen lips so perfect before. I wanted to *experience* those lips. I wanted to kiss Manny.

My thoughts were interrupted when the phone rang. It was his best friend calling to confirm their plans for later. During the conversation, I watched, I listened and I began to lose control. I gently kissed his arms. I was being shyly coy about it and thought that I could stop there. Manny began to give his friend a play-by-play report. Then I heard him say, "Yeah, man, she's asking for it."

As if common sense showed up for a visit—I got up and started to leave.

"After what she just started, she actually thinks she's going to walk out of here," he bragged. Then while still holding the phone,

Manny grabbed my arm.

Quickly he ended the call, "I'll catch you later, Nate."

While trying to exit I said, "It's getting late, I should go."

"So why were you kissing my arms?" he asked with a grin.

I didn't have an answer—my silence was a dead giveaway. He laid me gently back onto the bed and leaned over me.

"This is how it's done," he whispered.

Before I knew it, Manny was kissing me.

His tongue swam around mine. It was as if our mouths were made to connect. I pulled him closer while stroking his hair.

{"What are you doing?"}

That was a terrible time to hear that little voice inside myself again.

{"Olivia, you can't do this. He's using you and you know it."}

I wasn't going to let that voice ruin the moment that I had been waiting for all of my life. In all honesty, it was even more wonderful than I imagined. I started to feel as though I was floating, but things were moving too fast. I didn't want to be used, so I pulled away.

"I should really go. My mom is expecting me back soon. She's waiting for me right now," I lied.

"Did you think I was kidding? You're not going anywhere."

One might think that I was being forced to stay. But Manny's statement wasn't a demand; it was merely a fact. He knew that I wasn't going anywhere because he knew I never wanted to leave. From the moment we entered his room, I felt as though I had entered another galaxy. I felt as if I had survived a journey through a black hole and arrived in this parallel dimension on the other side. Through all of the rushing waves of emotions that overcame me, I felt safe. "You're not going anywhere" were the last words spoken for some time. Words were no longer needed.

As we gently touched and kissed, I learned so much about him. I began to feel as though I had known Manny all of my life. Nothing was said, but everything had been exposed. I finally knew that Manny felt strongly for me. The wondering was over.

As he walked me to the door, I felt weightless. By that time, we both knew what the other felt and neither of us had uttered a phrase.

"Call me later," Manny chimed.

"As soon as I get home," I told him.

I started my trek for home. While walking I screamed to myself, *I did it! I was right! He loves me too!*

{"Does he love you?"} The argument ensued.

Of course Manny loves me. I could feel it.

{"Are you sure love was what you were feeling or was it lust?"}

By this time, I really hated that voice and I knew it was wrong about this. Maybe there was lust between Manny and myself, but there was something much stronger as well. I was sure of it because the lust never fully took control. ***Manny and I didn't have sex.*** We didn't even remove our clothing. The rhythmic motion of his kiss and caress was so tender that we didn't have to do anything else. The fact that Manny didn't try to go any further revealed genuine sensitivity. I could tell that I was special to him.

{"Okay, Olivia, you're right you two didn't make love, but where do you go from here? What does this really mean?"}

I didn't know for sure, but I didn't mind taking the time to find out.

After returning home, I called Manny, and discovered that his parents had arrived home. (I was glad I left when I did.) His mother answered the phone and told me that Manny had just left. I assumed that he went to meet the friend who called earlier. I left a message with my phone number, but he didn't call back that night.

{"See, he's giving you the slip. You didn't mean as much as you thought."}

I wasn't going to believe that. I had spent my whole life dreaming about falling in love and being in love with the perfect guy.

So I thought to myself, *Maybe he's not completely perfect, but **I am in love**. And you don't just give up on love after one missed phone call.*

Chapter 6

The Turning Tides

Leaving Manny's house that day was the hardest thing I ever had to do. Part of me feared that I imagined the entire afternoon. The other part feared that I had actually lived the experience of being in his world, but that I'd never return. I started to think that maybe everything happened too easily and that maybe I was in for a cruel surprise. No matter what I was afraid of, I couldn't fight my feelings for him. Now that I'd held and kissed Manny, I couldn't just forget.

I'm more determined now than ever.

The next couple of weeks were exhilarating. Manny and I never really discussed our rendezvous. In class, we communicated, as usual, through glances, riddles and subliminal messages. Even though things didn't appear that much different on the outside, I was elated on the inside. I felt as if I were having the most romantic secret love affair. The secrecy of it all made it even more exciting. The entire situation motivated me. I began to feel a surge of creative energy. I started to take an interest in art and focused on the development of my drawing skills—what little I had, anyway. Manny's passion had ignited my own.

Unfortunately, years of watching soap operas have helped me to recognize when someone's flying high, they inevitably come crashing down. It didn't take long before I wanted more. Manny had become like some wonderful addiction. I wanted to go back into his world and I wanted to become a part of it. ***I needed to hear him invite me into his life and ask me to stay.*** I tried to broach the subject several times during our telephone conversations. Manny was very good at talking around the matter, but eventually he did tell me that he would be mine—exclusively—if I did one thing.

Before I let the cat out of the bag, I have to admit that I neglected to mention a vital part of this scenario—*my boyfriend.* Yes, at the time, I was dating someone. I truly didn't intend to hurt that person. Remember, I was only fantasizing about Manny. I never thought anything would happen between us. I know I shouldn't have even been dating someone if I had such strong feelings for someone else. I was just trying desperately to fill the void that my feelings for Manny had left. I originally thought that this person was a vague shadow of who Manny was. However, once I'd gotten to know more about both of them, I realized that they were nothing alike. By then, I had gotten even closer to Manny and my boyfriend had gotten even closer to me.

So here is Manny's request: "Break up with Josh."

That wasn't an unusual request. It only made his promise of exclusivity more plausible. So why not break up with my boyfriend when the only man I wanted was on the other end of the phone? I knew how much Josh cared for me. Even though I didn't return those feelings, I really didn't want to hurt him. This was not going to be easy.

The next day, I met Josh before school started to break the news to him. At first, I had decided to lie to him and not even mention Manny. There were other good reasons to end our relationship. We could never see each other without sneaking around and I hated that. Josh's mother wasn't very tolerant of interracial couples, Josh being Caucasian and I being African-American. Alone, that was a big enough reason to stop dating someone, and Manny didn't make things any easier. So why hurt Josh with the entire truth? Well, I always believed that lying to someone hurt him or her more than the truth ever could, so both truths came out.

"Josh, I don't know how to say this, but I don't think we should see each other anymore."

"Why?" Josh asked painfully.

Well, here goes. "It's more than just one thing. We're not good together. Your mom hates me—despite the fact that she's never met me! I can't even come to your house. The whole situation is really hard."

He broke in, "But we can work that out somehow. I could try to talk to her and maybe...."

"No Josh, you know how she feels. You can't compromise with someone who's a racist. I don't think you're going to change her mind and I don't want you to have to suffer for me."

"But I'd do anything for you. I love you, Olivia."

That was awful. I knew I had to tell him about Manny then. If I didn't, he was going to try any and everything to convince me to stay with him. I didn't want to drag it out.

"It's more than just your mom. Remember when you called my house a couple of weeks ago and I wasn't there. You said you got a little worried because I didn't come straight home from school."

"Yeah."

"I was with another guy—someone from art class. I went over his house and things got pretty intense."

"So, what do you mean? Did you have sex with him?" he asked angrily.

"No, actually, I didn't. We just kissed and kind of rolled around on his bed for a little while."

Tears began to swell up in his eyes.

"Oh, that's all, huh? You just rolled around on his bed and kissed! Well that's just great!" He was shouting by then.

"I didn't intend for anything to happen. You remember the guy I mentioned from my art class—"

"Him! Manny! You're still hung up on him!"

I had mentioned Manny to Josh earlier in our relationship when we were just friends. I had no idea that things were going to turn out like this.

The worst wasn't over. "I'm sorry, Josh. I really didn't want to hurt you. We started out just being friends and I want to stay friends. You are such a great guy; you're going to find someone to love."

Calmly, he replied, "I did—it was you."

I was so saddened that I ended the conversation and ran to the bathroom crying. I know that I didn't love Josh, but I wouldn't want to be treated the way I treated him and it hurt me to do it. What's that saying, "what goes around comes around"? Well, it came around rather quickly.

After school, I went to Manny's house to tell him the good news. Since I didn't see him in class earlier that day, I figured he stayed home again. When I arrived, he was alone, but something was different about him. Once inside, I hugged him. I related the story of how hard it was to hurt Josh, despite knowing it was the best thing for everyone involved. I was surprised by his reaction—or rather lack there of. Manny was so distant, not even allowing me to kiss him. I questioned him about his behavior, but only received a vague explanation. I was told that his life was suddenly overwhelming and too complicated.

"I just can't have a girlfriend right now."

"What?!" I was crushed. "What about the other day in your room? And why did you tell me to break up with Josh if you didn't want me?"

"I don't know. I guess I wanted to see if your feelings were real. I wanted to see if you were serious about me."

My mouth dropped open. "Great! You see that I'm serious about you and now you don't want us to be together! That doesn't make sense!"

"I just can't have a girlfriend right now. That doesn't mean I don't want you in my life."

I didn't know what changed, but that was it, *Manny wanted us to be friends*. At first, the irony of the whole thing made me laugh to myself. I remembered telling Josh the exact same thing earlier that day. I knew I deserved this.

"Fine. We can be friends," I told him indignantly. "But you're not getting rid of me that easily. You're going to realize that I'm good for you and when you're ready, they'll be nothing standing in our way."

After leaving his house, I only made it a few feet before I stopped and began weeping.

{"I told you that this would happen,"} the little voice whispered. {"You did your best, just let this go."}

Since I had come this far, I was not willing to turn back. Manny never said that he didn't care for me. He never told me that he didn't want to see me again, so there was still hope. I was determined not to give up on him so soon.

"We shared something in his room the other day and I could see in his eyes that there was something in him reaching out to me. He tried to repel me before and now he was pulling away again, but why?"

I didn't understand the abrupt turning of the tide, but I knew it wasn't over yet.

Chapter 7

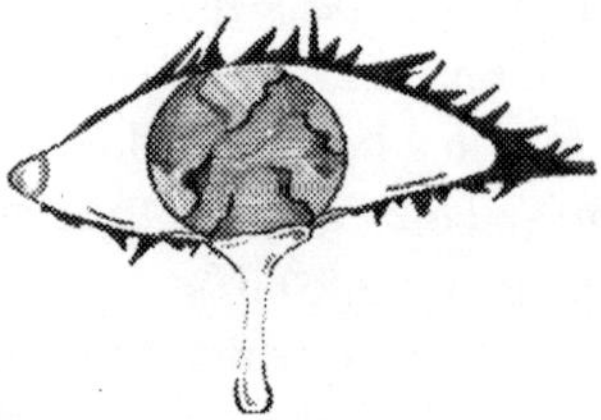

Leaving His World

The next couple of weeks were unusual. Manny was charming and sweet to me. I thought that things were going to turn around sooner than expected. Things took a turn—but for the worse!

One day in art class, I cornered Manny in the supply room. He had been somewhat withdrawn that day and I wanted to know if everything was all right.

"I haven't seen you in class the last couple of days. I call, but you're never home. I guess you're the type of guy who doesn't return phone calls."

"Sorry, I've been busy," he replied flatly.

Sweetly, I asked, "What's going on? You can tell me; I told you that I could be a good friend. There's no pressure."

Manny wouldn't look at me. All of a sudden he spoke, "I'm getting back with my ex-girlfriend."

"What?! After all of that crap you gave me about not being able to have a girlfriend because of your complicated life! Why are you doing this to me?!"

I tried not to raise my voice; I didn't want everyone in class to overhear. I was devastated enough without having eyewitnesses gossiping about it.

"Well, she kept calling me crying and telling me that she loves me and… I didn't know what else to do. I didn't want to hurt her."

"But hurting me is a lot easier, I guess." I was cold.

"It's not like that. Maybe if we had met before or at a different time and place we could have—"

"Forget it." My energy was drained.

I wanted to break down. I wanted to cry and scream and kick. But I wasn't going to let him know how destroyed I was. Fortunately, anger took over, allowing me to walk out of that room with *some* dignity. I was done trying to make a case for us. I was the only one fighting and I didn't even know what I was fighting against. I didn't mind the riddles. I could tolerate the mind games and cocky attitude. I could even understand why Manny wasn't in a good place to have more than a friendship. I could at the very least be his friend and support him through that rough time, but there was no way I was going to share him with some other girl! I wasn't going to hover around like some vulture, waiting for their relationship to expire so I could swoop down and devour the remains.

No thank you! I thought to myself. *I know I deserve better than that!*

I turned and walked out of the supply room and left class, barely able to hold back my tears. As it turned out, that day was officially the day that I left his world. Manny never returned to class. I found out later that he had left school permanently. I didn't know the details and I didn't want to know. Actually, I was relieved since I didn't have to suffer through the rest of the school year being constantly reminded of the extreme rejection I endured.

The fantasy I lived was fleeting, Manny was gone and I wasn't going to see him again, I said to myself.

{"It's for the best."} This time the voice was kind and comforting. This time, I agreed with it.

So it was over and somehow I managed to resume living. Somehow I was able to move on. Every day that passed was a day the pain lessened. Subsequently, I realized that I still loved Manny and always would, but that didn't matter anymore. You can love someone so much that they disappear. The person you love is no longer there and the person that's left couldn't care less. I still believed that there was something between us. He denied it, fought it and ran away from it, but that was his loss.

A year later, it became someone else's gain. ***Then the phone rang.***

Chapter 8

The Other End of the Line

A lot had changed since the last time I heard his voice.

My mother and I moved into a house of our own. I'd been maintaining a 3.8 grade point average while preparing to take the college entrance exams. I was also working part-time and had been steadily dating someone for three months. His name was Malcolm Lewis. Ironically, I met him while participating in some other form of "well-rounded curriculum." I was on a golf team with his sister. One day, it was her turn to arrange a ride for us to get to practice; as it turned out, she recruited her brother for the job.

My first impression of him was not favorable. He seemed pretty crabby, actually. I found out later that he'd been dragged out of bed to chauffeur his sister and me—of course he was not happy about it. I didn't think much of our encounter, but his sister was driving me crazy with accusations of a love connection. For some reason, she thought he liked me. However, I couldn't see how she reached that conclusion from a fifteen-minute trip to a golf course.

"No, silly," she said, laughing. "Malcolm has seen you before."

"What? I've never met your brother before today."

"I know you haven't *officially met* him, but *he's seen you before.*"

The whole conversation seemed ridiculous to me. Malcolm was no longer in high school. He was definitely what one would call "an older guy," being four years my senior. So I was amazed at the thought of him ever seeing me before. I was sure that we did not move in the same circles.

"He sees you practically every day, walking to work."

After thinking about it, I realized that Malcolm and his sister, Renee, lived down the street from our new house. I walked down that street every single day to go to work at the fast food restaurant at the end of the block. I suddenly remembered that I had seen a guy in a doorway before. He smiled at me and said "Hello," and I did the same. The pieces were starting to fit.

"No! He's actually seen me in my uniform walking to work! Well, there you go then! I doubt seriously if that picture of me would have turned your brother's head."

"I know my brother, and he likes you, I'm sure of it!"

The conversation continued throughout practice. It was fun to think that an older guy was interested in me, especially after everything I'd been through.

During the year after Manny walked out of my life, I began making some very poor decisions. I regret to admit that two guys who I thought cared about me had duped me. I dated the first for a couple of months, allowing myself to believe that he was actually falling in love with me. After having sex with him, I was devastated to hear that out of the blue, he decided things weren't working out between us anymore.

{"How stupid are you? First you convince yourself that Manùel Nelson was falling for you and then you continue your disillusionment with this guy! At least you were smart enough to use protection."}

My self-esteem was being annihilated. I suppose I just wanted to feel safe, loved and cherished, the same as I felt during the brief time I spent in Manny's life. I longed for that feeling so much that I looked for it in all the wrong places.

Months passed after that horrible situation, but yet again I ended up experiencing another humiliating blow to my sense of worth. I thought I had met a great guy. He was sweet and funny and cute. We seemed to be getting along beautifully and then *it* happened, we became intimate. However, this time I wasn't looking for love, I was looking to forget. I was tired of getting caught up in some emotional whirlwind just to end up empty and alone. I decided not to seek out a committed relationship or a passionate love affair. Even with that thought in mind, I was shocked to discover that "the great guy" I was seeing was the best friend of the guy whom I thought really cared for me, then dumped me after getting what he wanted. Basically, "the great guy" was only after what his friend had bragged about.

After Manny and those two guys, I just gave up on the idea of loving anyone or anyone loving me. I was sure all of the soap operas were right. Two people meet, get excited about the "newness" of each other, fall in love, make love, and then fall out of love, just to end up hating each other or simply moving on to the next "new" person.

{"Real love doesn't exist. If it did, you'd never find it, because it's the most elusive thing God created."} That voice was always there. Through good or bad times I could always count on it.

So by the time this conversation had arisen about Malcolm, I was more than skeptical. It had been a little over a year since Manny walked out of my life and a matter of months since all of that other stuff happened. I wasn't ready to go through anymore with anyone else. Nevertheless, "ready or not—here it comes."

Malcolm picked us up from golf practice and I went back to their house to try on some clothes that Renee *just happened* to want to give me that day. There is where it all began.

I was surprised by Malcolm's charming nature. He was coy, funny and very sweet. We had been talking for only a short while when he asked me for my phone number. I found out later that his sister had already given him my number, but he wanted to ask my permission before calling me. He offered to drive me home, but since it was just down the street, I insisted on walking. Kindly, Malcolm walked me to the door and actually kissed my hand as I exited. I have to admit, I was impressed.

The next couple of months were grand. Even though I had to keep Malcolm's real age quiet, telling my mother that he was only nineteen, she learned to like him and so did I. He was always such a gentleman. He owned a car, went to college and worked nights. Regardless of how busy he was, Malcolm always managed to make time for me, calling every night. Eventually, I let my guard down. I began to feel things for Malcolm; I began to trust him. As time passed, he permeated every aspect of my life. Ultimately, our relationship reached the level of intimacy. By then, I felt confident about "us." We had waited for months and our relationship seemed more solid than any I had ever been involved in. Our union provided me with the security and the happiness that I had always wanted. Even after we had sex, Malcolm and I seemed stronger than ever.

Sadly, though, our bond did begin to deteriorate. Little by little, Malcolm didn't have time for me the way he once did. On top of that, when we did find time to be together we would argue. To my knowledge we were just a couple experiencing a few problems, but then something happened that would send this relationship spiraling to its end. What happened? *Manny happened.* This brings me to the day the phone rang.

Despite the fact that my mom and I had moved, we decided to keep our old phone number. We thought it was not worth the trouble of changing it if we didn't have to. Who knew that one little choice was going to change life as I knew it?

"Hello?"

"Hello." I recognized his voice instantly.

"Hi, can I speak to Olivia?"

"Speaking."

"Do you know who this is?"

I thought to myself, *What a dumb question, how could I possibly forget his voice?*

"Yes, this is Manùel, isn't it?"

"You remembered."

"How could I forget?"

I was confident. I was over him, and whatever the reason was for this phone call, it wouldn't change anything. Or would it?

Chapter 9

The Manny I Never Knew

Hearing Manny's voice again sent chills up my spine. I thought I'd never hear from or see him again. During the entire conversation, I was pleasant and cheerful. I wasn't angry with him. How could I be? ***I loved him.*** Even though that love wasn't enough to hold us together, I knew that it meant something.

Our talk was light-hearted and refreshing. He told me that he had misplaced my number and it took him a year to find it!

"You've actually been looking for my number all of this time?"

"Well maybe not the entire time, but I'm glad I found it."

I didn't know what was happening. Manny sounded so different—almost as if he were flirting with me. But that couldn't be the case because he could have any woman he wanted and he chose someone else, right?

In fact, there were no riddles and no subliminal messages. Manny and I had the best conversation ever. I told him about my new boyfriend and he told me how things didn't work out with his girlfriend. At the time, that information didn't send a signal to my brain. From what I could make out of the entire conversation, we were old friends talking about old times. Manny never suggested I leave my boyfriend; in fact, he said he was happy for me. He told me how he'd been having family problems and that he had been kicked out of his house. He revealed that he had just been allowed to move back into his parents' house just a couple of months prior to this phone call. After hearing about his experiences as a drifter and practically a homeless person, I could understand how and why we lost touch. By the time our exchange ended, I was truly glad that Manny called. I didn't expect much more than what I received that day. He gave me his phone number again and I told him that we'd keep in touch. I didn't think we really would, but I was wrong.

As the weeks passed, Manny and I spoke on the phone every day. He became my best friend. I could tell him anything. The entire experience was strange, since our relationship started out with riddles and mind games. Now it was turning into long talks, revealing secrets and sharing stories. I had never felt so connected to another human being.

During this time, things really changed—not just between Manny and me, but also between Malcolm and me. I was clear with Manny about my feelings for my boyfriend, and he never pressured me to change those feelings. So when problems between Malcolm and I worsened, Manny was my shoulder to cry on. He was very supportive and kind, never judgmental or critical and always attentive. That was Malcolm's entire problem; he was no longer any of those things. He became just the opposite, no longer attentive and very critical. I was getting fed up with his excuses for breaking our dates and not calling. Slowly, those nightly calls from Malcolm were being replaced with nightly calls from Manny, but I didn't mind. With every disappointment received from Malcolm, Manny was there to rebound it. Everything seemed to be falling apart and coming together all at the same time.

The final defeat for Malcolm occurred when I became very ill. Apparently, studying, working and going to school didn't mix well with dieting. I'm not sure if those things were the direct cause of my illness, but they didn't help any. At first, I was diagnosed with tonsillitis. I had severe throat pain, a high fever and a terrible earache. After going to the emergency room, I was given an ineffective antibiotic. Days later, I went to my family doctor where it was discovered that I had an abscess on my left tonsil. I was sent, immediately, by the physician, to the hospital and admitted the same day. I thought everyone was being overly protective until I was told that surgery was scheduled for the next day. The abscess had to be lanced and the fluid drained or it could burst and poison my bloodstream, similar to appendicitis. I then became frightened.

Although my mother visited me during the day, the night was the loneliest, until I received a call from…Manny. He had called my house asking to speak to me. My mother told him that I was in the hospital and gave him the number to my room. When the phone rang, I didn't expect to hear Manny's voice. I thought my boyfriend was going to check in. He had only spoken to me once and that was earlier in the day. I figured that he couldn't go to sleep without telling me good night, but after answering the phone, I realized that he could.

"Hi, Olivia."

"Manny?"

"How are you? Your mom told me you were really sick."

The concern in his voice was refreshing. As we talked, I began to feel as if I was being rescued from my fears. Although it was painful to speak, I explained the procedure I would be undergoing and told him that I couldn't sleep. He told me that he would talk to me all night if he had to, just to make me feel better—and he did. He told a fabulous tale of forbidden love. The story was sad and yet it made me feel uplifted, because I believed that Manny was giving me another riddle and that he was trying to reveal—without revealing—that *he* was the one who fell in love with someone already taken—me. After listening to his comforting voice, I was finally able to sleep.

Early the next morning, I was taken into surgery. The procedure went as planned. By the evening, I was up for visitors. Guess who arrived? Malcolm! He showed up with a stuffed animal and an explanation of his whereabouts. He said that his mother was not well and he didn't know who to spend time with. Ultimately, his mother's illness won out over mine. That was totally understandable, but that didn't excuse the fact that he hadn't at least called the night before. During the visit, Malcolm was kind and sympathetic, but it was too little, too late. I had already decided to break up with him. I was tired of not being a priority to him and I began to think that maybe he wasn't always being honest with me. Breaking up with someone is always difficult. Since I couldn't speak very much after surgery, I decided to wait until I was feeling better and could verbalize my feelings more effectively.

Regardless of when I planned to tell Malcolm, I told Manny my decision that night. Of course, he called to make sure I got out of surgery okay and to tell me that he wanted to visit me in the hospital. I may have neglected to mention the fact that Manny and I had not *seen* each other in a year and a half. We had been talking on the phone for a couple of months, but we had not come face to face, as of yet. After all of that time, there was no way I was going to let him see me laying in a hospital bed like that!

"No, Manny, I don't want you to come visit me while I'm in here!" I struggled to scream.

"Calm down, Olivia, and tell me why not."

"I look horrible! Please don't come here!"

"I'm sure you look beautiful," he said softly.

Then I knew everything I had felt for him was still there, but now it was multiplied by a hundred!

"Please, if I'm your friend, just wait until I'm better. We'll set up a time to meet and we'll go out or something. Please!"

"Okay, but as soon as you're better, you're all mine."

That was subliminal. He didn't have to say "you're all mine," but he did, because he wanted me to hear those words and understand the hidden meaning behind them.

{"Olivia, what are you doing?"}

I hadn't heard that voice in a while. There must have been a warning light that went off in my head to alert it to danger.

I'm falling in love, all over again!

{"I know. Do you think that's wise?"}

This time is different because Manny is different. We've shared so many things with each other. I trust him and I know he trusts me.

{"I hope you're right, because you worked so hard to get over him before."}

Things have changed and so have I. It's going to work out this time. I was certain.

Manny had been open and honest with me, while Malcolm was

becoming increasingly evasive. I knew whom I could believe in and whom I could confide in, now I had to make it official. I had to make some needed changes in my life and I was prepared to let Malcolm know that he was no longer included.

I wasn't being naïve. I didn't expect Manny and I to declare our undying love to each other, then run off into the sunset. I was just glad that he was there for me. I would have been content with the way things were going, but all of a sudden the pace of the situation took off like a rocket!

Chapter 10

The Journal—Part Two

Dear Journal,

I can't believe I've been spending my day thinking of my beginning with Manny. I shouldn't be thinking of anyone except my husband, but I can't help it. Ever since I started accepting visits from him, I can't stop thinking about our tumultuous past and our passionate encounters. His presence has also brought many memories of my teenage years spiraling back to me like a doomed 757 taking a nosedive into the ocean! I've been in reflection now for weeks.

Today, I started thinking of how at the age of 16 and a half, I felt as if I had already lived the life of a thirty-year-old. Throughout the several years when I watched my mom be abused, the numerous times we fled for our lives in the midst of a cold night and the various stays at shelters for battered women and children, I had no time to enjoy my innocence. Friends were few—if any. It's hard to make and keep them when you're constantly being uprooted. My mom would leave the chaos of violence that my father's presence would bring, but if he didn't find us, she'd eventually gravitate back to him. He would re-make promises that she had previously hoped in. Then his true identity would resurface. He'd start drinking, smoking marijuana and beating my mom, not to mention neglecting me. By then, we would all be moved in together and trapped into the cycle of brutality again. I'm sure my brother and sister were glad they had a different father and wished they could have been with him instead. I always wished that myself.

Of course my self-esteem had always been low. Why wouldn't it be? I figured if a girl's own daddy couldn't love her and cherish her, why would any other man? So I destructively allowed myself to be taken advantage of. From as young as 14, I sought the love of a father by losing my virginity to a young man who promised to love me forever. At the time, I felt mature enough to handle the situation, but afterward, I was reduced to emotions of a mere adolescent. I wasn't ready for what a sexual relationship had to offer—good or bad—I was a lost child who so desperately wanted to be found. I wasn't looking for sex; I was looking for safety and security in the arms of a gentle, yet strong male figure. Sex just happened to be an unwanted byproduct of my search.

The fact that I was molested for many years only added to the trauma of having my tender years ripped away from me. I can't even recall when it began or when it finally ended. Sometimes, I am plagued by images that reveal the disgusting sexual acts that I endured as a small child. I thank God that I can't remember much more.

Although my upbringing could be classified as disastrous, I don't blame all of my mistakes on it. I am aware of right and wrong and I know how to take responsibility for my failures.

I've begun a journey inside myself that will hopefully end with an absolution. I don't want to hurt my husband, but I'm drawn to Manny and the feelings he evokes in me. Maybe I could learn from my mistakes and move on—a better person. I would rather fight for love than be defeated by it. That's why I can't stop thinking about him. Especially about the first day we met, after over a year of being apart....

Chapter 11

Today We Meet

"Hello?"

"Hello, Malcolm," I said plainly.

"Olivia, how are you?"

"I'm much better, thanks for asking." I was indignant. "You know, I was released from the hospital several days ago. I thought I would have heard from you by now."

"Oh, well, um…I've been busy."

"You've been busy a lot lately, haven't you? In fact, before I got sick, you were always busy with work or school or something. Personally, I think you're just too busy for the added responsibility of a girlfriend." I was cold.

"What do you mean by that?"

"I'm tired of not being high on your list of priorities. Most importantly, I'm tired of your lies!"

"Lies? When have I lied to you?"

"For starters, every promise you've made to me lately has gone unfulfilled. Since you've developed a pretty distinct pattern, all of your new promises are classified as lies to me. But here's a better example: I found out that you haven't been enrolled at the university for months. You've been lying to me about attending classes all this time! So, if you haven't been busy with school, I wonder what's been preoccupying your time?"

Malcolm cut in, "Wait a minute, I can explain that!"

"Don't bother," I rebuked. "I also found out that the little family vacation you told me you were taking last month never happened!

The next time you lie to me and you don't want me to find out, maybe you should let everyone else know the score so they won't blow it for you!"

"What's that supposed to mean?"

"A couple of days before I ended up in the hospital, I asked your sister how she enjoyed going to Chicago with you and your mom. Unfortunately, she was oblivious to what I was referring to and blew your cover. She told me that none of you left town that weekend! I would ask what you were doing the whole time when I thought you were innocently vacationing with your family, but I don't give a damn!"

"Olivia, I can explain. I just needed some time to myself and I didn't know how to tell you."

"I trusted you, Malcolm. All you had to do was be honest with me. How do you think I felt when I found out that you've been lying to me? I couldn't even talk to you when these revelations fell into my lap! You were nowhere to be found! So don't worry, Malcolm, you can have all the time you need. It's over."

"Wait, I know things haven't been going that well with us lately, but we can work on it—I just need time."

"I know, you already said that! So you take all the time you need, but ***we're*** out of time!"

CLICK!

This is the beginning of a new Olivia, I thought to myself, smiling inside.

Moments later the phone rang. I was afraid that Malcolm was calling back to state a newly revised case for us. Yet, upon answering the call, I was pleasantly surprised.

"Hello?"

"Olivia, it's me."

"Me, who?" I joked, since I could recognize his voice anywhere.

"Manny, of course." He was flirting with me, I could tell.

"I knew that," I said, flirting back.

"So, when can I see you?"

"How about today? My day has been all cleared."

"Today sounds great! What time?"

"How about four o'clock? That gives me a few hours to get ready for this momentous occasion."

"I'll be there."

After giving him directions to my house, we cheerfully said our good-byes. The house was ours for the evening, so we'd be alone for the first time since the last time I visited his home, so long ago. I was so excited I could barely stand it.

Manny and I had been talking on the phone for several weeks and I finally felt that we had begun to build a relationship on solid ground. There were no more riddles, no more subliminal messages and no more rejections. We had actually become good friends. I loved talking with him more than anything. I learned so much about Manny's dreams and his nightmares. He aspired to artistic greatness, but was haunted by terrible visions in his sleep.

Manny revealed to me how he would wake up terrified and drenched in sweat. He described his nightmares as being "homicidal aftermath" or "vivid images of a brutal crime scene." When talking about those dreams, Manny's voice would get low and soft, almost as if he didn't want to hear his own words speak of them. I asked him why he had such gruesome dreams but he never had an answer.

Manny had become an open book on many subjects; on the other hand, he could also be vague and obscure. In fact, whenever the discussion turned towards his parents or his home life, he would quickly but subtly divert my attention elsewhere. The more we talked, the more I got the feeling he was hiding something from me.

{"Maybe he's got a girlfriend or a baby he's not telling you about."} Once again, that voice warned me away from Manùel Nelson.

It's deeper than that, I thought. *Something so painful and even so terrible that he just* ***can't*** *tell me.*

{"Maybe he doesn't want you to know."}

Or maybe he's afraid of what would happen if I found out.

At that point I realized that Manny and I never discussed why he originally rejected me or why he suddenly came back into my life.

When our conversations got too deep, the walls went up around him.

I don't care! There's a beauty and innocence in him that I'm drawn too. He'll disclose everything when he's ready.

{"I hope so, Olivia. He hurt you so badly before and that's when you barely knew him. Now things have gone so far that he could cut your heart out."}

KNOCK, KNOCK!

The sound shook me from my thoughts. I looked out the window. It was him! Manny was standing right outside my door! I savored the moment briefly, although I didn't want to keep him waiting for too long. Slowly, I began to open the door. Seconds later, our eyes met. We smiled at each other.

"Hi, Olivia." His voice was deep and soft.

I could feel myself blushing. "Hi, Manny."

I was instantly swept away. He was more gorgeous than I remembered. His hair had grown so long that it actually touched his shoulders! I barely recognized him because he had become a titanic mass of muscle! His physique was even more chiseled than before. I guess I got caught up in the moment because all of a sudden I heard....

"Can I come in?"

"Oh, um...of course, come in."

He walked by me leaving behind a magnificent scent. *He even smells sexy!* I secretly said to myself.

Instantly, I felt weak. Suddenly, a hot spring erupted between my legs. I desperately fought to hide my embarrassment. I honestly didn't want to lose control.

Today we meet, who knows about tomorrow? But nothing more today—NOTHING MORE! I thought.

My tempest of emotion must have shown up on my face.

"Olivia, are you okay?" he asked softly.

{"SNAP OUT OF IT!"} that voice yelled, jarring me from my trance.

"I'm fine," spilled out from my lips. "Did you have a hard time finding me?"

"No, not at all. I'll always find you, Olivia, wherever you are."

My heart was hammering. {"Say something else!"}

"So are you thirsty or hungry? Do you want me to get you anything?" I nervously uttered.

While taking off his coat, Manny said, "All I want is for you to come over to me."

I walked over to him slowly. He reached out his hand and pulled me to him. Before I knew it, I was in Manny's arms—the first time since that historic day in his room. He gave me the warmest hug. I was still in his arms when he whispered, "I've missed you so much."

The hot spring turned into a waterfall. At the same time, I felt truly happy to see the friend I'd been sharing the phone lines with every night for so many weeks.

"I missed you too…." My words were interrupted when Manny placed his soft lips over mine, giving me the sweetest kiss I'd ever felt. Moments passed, turning that soft kiss into a very passionate one. Nevertheless, we slowly released our grasp on one another. I got the feeling that Manny was trying to be just as cautious as I was. We sat down on the couch, but since I wasn't sure what to say to him, I anxiously sprang from my seat.

"Let me show you around," I said while guiding him to the kitchen. I gave him a thorough tour that ended in the basement.

"It's great that you and your mom finally have a house of your own."

"Thanks. I was so used to living in an apartment or duplex that sometimes I still think I hear footsteps on the ceiling."

Manny smiled and took my hand again. "Let's go upstairs."

By the time we made it back to the couch, I was much more relaxed. I started to remember that Manny was still the person I'd been confiding in. Softly, I admitted, "I finally broke up with Malcolm."

"It took you long enough," he said with a grin.

I could feel myself blushing again when I asked, "What do you mean by that?"

"Well, I know you left Malcolm because he wasn't treating you right, but I think you broke up with him for another reason too."

"Yeah, and what's that?"

"You finally realized that you belong to me—you always have."

"What?" I laughed. "You make it sound like I'm your property or something?"

"*Something like that,*" he said confidently. "The fact is we belong to each other."

"Why are you saying these things? I thought you just wanted to be friends! Last year you totally destroyed me and went back to your ex-girlfriend. Why should I believe you now?" I started to remember my pain.

"That's been over for a very long time. I only did that because that was the *only thing I* ***could*** *do*."

I was dumbfounded. "Now, what's that supposed to mean?"

"Olivia, I know there's a lot you don't understand about me, but I can say the same about you!"

"What?" I was stunned.

"Why were you chasing me? Why didn't you give up on me?"

"Wait a minute, I gave up and then I moved on! I hadn't seen you in a year and then out of the blue you called me, remember?"

"I know."

I could tell that he sensed my anger.

"Why did you call me anyway? What do you want from me?"

"I couldn't forget about you—no matter how hard I tried. I had to see you again. I looked everywhere for your number. I almost went up to the school to look for you, but I found it before I had to go that far."

"Why? Why would you go through so much trouble for a girl you tried so hard to get rid of?"

"I've spent the past year thinking of the way you would watch me from across the classroom. How you would smile at me and how you stood by me as a friend no matter how much I pushed you away…."

"Yeah, and you repaid me by going to some other girl and then dropping off the face of the earth!"

"I'm sorry, Olivia." Manny's head dropped and his voice lowered.

"No matter what happened, I never stopped loving you."

{"What did he say?"} That voice rang in my ears. But I was too astounded to speak.

"I love you and if you give me the chance I can make up for everything I did to hurt you. Please let me have the chance."

Manny was saying all the words that I desperately wanted to hear.

"But if you loved me before, why did you walk out on me, how could you hurt me like that?"

"I can't explain all of that right now, but I'm here and I promise that I won't ever leave you again."

{"What the heck is going on here?"}

I'm finally living my dream, I answered the voice.

{"Just be careful, Olivia. When something seems too good to be true, it usually is."}

I started to question him further, but I had never heard him verbalize his feelings for me. So I decided to give him the opportunity to prove that his words were true. Besides, at that point, I was so swept away by Manny's presence, I couldn't protest.

Just when I began to speak once again, my words were stopped with a kiss. When he finally released his tender grip on my mouth, I was only able to say, "*I love you.*"

Manny replied, "I know, and you're the only one who ever has."

That evening marked the beginning of our saga.

Chapter 12

Two Become One

Officially, Manny and I were together. Before that time, I couldn't remember being any happier. We spent our days together talking, laughing and growing in love. During our numerous talks and visits, Manny would slowly peek out from behind his self-built walls and reveal things about himself and his past.

I finally found out why Manny left school last year; it was due to a grave injustice that was committed against him. He gave up trusting or putting faith in anyone, deciding that he could only rely upon himself.

He had been entered into a major art contest with the first prize being a scholarship to Detroit's prestigious institute of higher learning for the most creative and artistic, College for Creative Studies. Also included in the prize were art supplies, an art table and even a hefty monetary award. Manny's surrealistic illustrations astounded the judges—he came in first place! He all but had the check in his hand when he received a horrifying revelation.

"My art teacher didn't fill out the entry forms right, so technically I was not entered." Manny's voice was sullen. "The official decision came down moments later, everything I had won was stripped from me and given to the guy who came in second place. I was devastated! I couldn't understand how that teacher could have been so incompetent, so I confronted him later that day in his classroom. He actually tried to blame me! I had already spoken to the judges and they told me that the mistake was officially the fault of the art teacher who didn't follow the contest's entry rules. When I gave my teacher that information, his reply was simply, 'We'll do it again next year.' I told him that I wouldn't be around next year for him to screw up again and that I was tired of him using me to make him look like a good art teacher—when he didn't even know how to draw! I was better than him and everyone who saw my work knew it. Maybe that's why he didn't care that I lost my scholarship. He didn't even try to apologize and that made me even more furious. All I could see was red. I felt the blood boiling in my veins. Before I knew it, I had knocked all the stuff on his desk to the floor and stormed out, slamming the door behind me. The door crashed shut and the glass shattered."

While telling the story, Manny was eerily calm. The entire experience obviously hardened him. And that was only the beginning.

"What did your parents say about all of that, didn't they try to get that teacher fired or challenge the judges' decision?" I was hoping he wouldn't avoid the question, as was his previous practice whenever the subject turned toward his parents.

"Yeah, maybe they would have done something...if they cared." Manny's voice revealed his pain. "They didn't do anything, so that bastard got away with not doing his job—not a damn thing happened to him!" His anger surfaced.

I hesitated, but I asked anyway, "I just don't understand why didn't they ***do*** anything."

"I told you, they just don't care! I've been seriously drawing since I was nine years old—and I don't mean cartoon characters either! At the age of nine, my work was being mistaken for something one of my uncles could have drawn. That was a great compliment to me because they were my artistic role models. I mean, they never had any formal training and they didn't illustrate for a living, but their sophisticated styles motivated me to work harder. By the time I reached the age of fifteen, I was able to draw better than both of my uncles put together. Despite that fact, my father would use drawings that I had spent hours working on as a place to sit his coffee, staining and ruining the entire piece."

"I can't believe that your dad was so hurtful to you. Well, what about your mom, has she ever encouraged you or tried to talk to your father about your talent?"

"Sometimes my mom comments on my drawings but usually she's not too interested in what I'm into. Besides, if she does attempt to approach my father about the way he treats me, a huge argument flares up."

"Do you and your father fight a lot?"

"I guess you can say that, since most of the time I don't even see it coming."

"Well, what do you usually fight about?"

"My friends."

"What's wrong with your friends? You're not in a gang or anything, right?"

"No. They're not in a gang, they're just the wrong color."

"What?" I was afraid of where this was going.

"To my father, my friends are 'niggers' and I shouldn't waste time with them."

"I can't believe that! There are still people who feel that way about African-Americans?" I was shocked.

"Well, pretty much all of my family."

"What? Even your mom? But she's a minority too—she's Mexican, right?"

"Yeah, but from what they tell me, that's how they were raised and that's just the way they are. We live in a predominantly black neighborhood, and even though they get along with people in the area, they would prefer I don't bring them to the house."

My mouth dropped open. "Oh, my God! That's why when I met your dad the other day, he looked at me like I had three eyes and an antenna! I felt so awkward, but I thought I was overreacting. Man, was I wrong! Well, did he say anything about me after I left?"

"No, not yet. Usually he gives me grief over my friend, Nate. He's like a brother to me and he's black. Well, actually, he's mixed, but it doesn't matter. He's partly black and that's enough for my parents. They think they have all kinds of reasons for not liking him; really the whole situation is pretty complicated and intense."

We talked for quite a while about Manny's home life. The conversation seemed to drain him, but I could tell that he felt relief. Unfortunately, I also got the feeling that he was still withholding some information, almost as if he were trying not to tell me too much.

"What does this mean for us? If your parents hate your black friends, they must despise your black girlfriend!"

"Don't worry about that. I can handle my parents." Once again, Manny's voice was eerily calm—even chilling.

"I can't believe this is happening again! Josh's mom wouldn't tolerate him dating a black girl either and I didn't want him going up against her for my sake. I definitely don't want you to endure your parents' wrath for me; I'm just not worth the struggle. "

"Don't you ever say that! You're more than worth it! Besides, I'll be moving out on my own soon, then they'll be nothing stopping us." Manny sounded determined, but I sensed a touch of uncertainty.

I didn't push the issue. I just wanted to enjoy Manny while he was there in my arms. I believed in his conviction to not let anything come between us, so I didn't object when he was ready to talk about something else.

We made great strides that day. He opened up to me in ways that I never thought he would and I was sure that was just the beginning.

After pulling me close and kissing me good-bye, Manny promised to return tomorrow.

The next day turned out to be unlike any other. When Manny arrived in the early afternoon, he was riding a motor scooter called a "Helix." When I heard an engine roar up the side of the house, I was shocked to discover Manny sitting on a cherry red clap of thunder! It was beautiful! He mentioned to me that he bought it used right before the beginning of winter. That day was the first time he'd taken it out of storage in months.

"Would you like to hop on and have a ride?" he asked, smiling sweetly.

"Well, I am tempted, but how about after lunch, I've got everything waiting." I was a little intimidated by that machine; I'd never ridden on a motorcycle before.

"Alright, but I will get you on here with me, right?"

"I promise."

We came inside and had a wonderful time together. After lunch, I persuaded Manny to clean up our dishes while I jumped into the shower and changed for our bike ride. He was more than happy to oblige.

While showering, I heard a knock at the bathroom door.

"Yes?" I yelled over the noise of the running water.

The door creaked as it slowly opened.

"Olivia, I can't find the scouring powder…." Manny's voice trailed off. I realized that he was staring at my nude silhouette through the shower's glass door.

"Manny?"

After a brief pause, I finally heard, "Uh, yeah?"

"What are you doing, peeping?"

"I'm not peeping, I'm staring." He chuckled softly.

"I thought you were looking for the scouring powder. It's under the kitchen sink."

Again, there was nothing but silence. Finally, I saw the door close and heard it shut behind Manny as he left.

That was weird, I thought. *Manny practically saw me naked and then he turned and walked away.*

{"Maybe he didn't like what he saw."} That voice could really be a pain sometimes.

Or maybe he's just a complete gentleman.

I hurried out of the shower and found Manny sitting at the kitchen table.

"The kitchen looks great! Thanks for washing the dishes for me."

Manny's eyes were intense; he didn't speak. I suddenly realized that I rushed out of the bathroom so quickly that I only put on my robe. I was standing in front of Manny and it felt like he could see right through the terrycloth. He got up from his seat and walked over to me.

"Are you feeling okay? You haven't said a word since you came into the bathroom and asked about the scouring powder."

More silence. He pulled me closer to him, brushing his lips across mine. Gradually, his delicate kiss turned into a passionate, heated exchange. That was the catalyst that led to his sweeping me off of my feet. I was being carried to my bedroom. Upon entering the room, I whispered, "What are you doing?"

While laying me on the bed, Manny finally said, "I just need to look at you."

"Look at me?"

Slowly, Manny opened my robe.

"I just want to see your beautiful brown skin."

Before the words had fully escaped his lips, I was revealed in front of him.

Manny's hands reached out to survey. Although, they were coarse from working as a laborer, his touch was unexpectedly soft. Gently, his hands roamed across my skin, exploring the hills, valleys and crevices. Those hands were searching more than my body; they were searching my soul. I didn't speak. I watched his eyes; they revealed his thoughts. He was savoring every moment and so was I. We both knew what was going to happen next, and we were both powerless to stop it.

I had been so afraid that Manny was going to break my heart again, but at that moment I felt as if he was incapable of doing so. I had finally been invited into his world and I was a very welcomed guest. Our relationship had become deeply rooted. We had unmasked our secrets and our hopes, revealing more to each other than to anyone else on earth. Our senses were heightened and in tune to one another. The time had arrived to fuse our lost hearts together—two became one.

Gradually, Manny bared himself to me. I lay there watching him remove his shirt; his pants followed. (I found out later that he never wore underwear—that day was no exception!) Time seemed to stand still. I was motionless as he sat beside me and completely removed my robe. The intensity of the moment was electrifying.

Finally, the silence was broken. As we sat enthralled by each other's nakedness, Manny spoke. "I've never seen a woman with such an unusual skin tone. It looks like creamy, melted caramel."

"I've never been compared to caramel before," I said, smiling.

"Why not? You're definitely sweet enough." Manny smiled back.

He leaned over me and instantly we began to kiss wildly.

Suddenly, he pulled away.

"I love you, Olivia," Manny whispered. "I never meant to hurt you."

It was as if he felt pain at that moment—pain for having caused me pain.

He continued, "I've never known anyone like you before. I've never known anyone who makes me feel the way you do."

Manny appeared as if he were meticulously treasuring every moment. Seconds later, he was on top of me. Again we began kissing uncontrollably. Soon, Manny was emotionally and physically inside of me. Rhythmically, he moved between my thighs while gently kissing my neck and shoulders. Before that moment, I had never experienced that level of ecstasy. Every move he made was graceful. We glided through the sheets like synchronized swimmers through the watery deep. He was leading the dance, but ultimately I was able to follow every movement with precision. He wasn't making love to me; we were making love to each other. I could feel his heart pounding inside of his chest.

"You're so beautiful," floated from Manny's lips.

I'd never heard of any man speaking to a woman so sweetly and lovingly while in the midst of passion.

Throughout our intimate encounter, Manny was intensely gentle and overwhelmingly adoring. His stamina was unyielding; his energy was unstoppable; his love was unmistakable.

Light turned into darkness. Our rapturous delight eventually reached its climax and then gradually came to an end—hours after it began. I had never experienced intimacy that beautiful, extreme or overpowering. Afterward, I lay naked and motionless in his arms. Neither of us uttered a sound. Our time together drew to a close. Achingly, we dressed and parted.

Chapter 13

The Journal—Part Three

Dear Journal,

My conflict has deepened. Last night my husband and I had another heated argument. It was the usual debate: He thinks I'm selfish and I think he's self-absorbed! He told me that I should be more accommodating of his needs since I stay at home and he works all day. Suffice it to say, he's the one who insisted I become a housewife and one day, a stay-home mom. He would tell me that he always wanted to take care of me and allow me to pursue all of my dreams and desires. He also told me that he worried about me a lot and he didn't like the idea of my having to drive to work alone every day. "What would I do if you got into an accident or someone tried to assault you? I couldn't live if I lost you," he would say. I believed him at the time. Now I'm starting to think that maybe he just wanted to keep me hidden away on a shelf, only to be retrieved upon his request. Why wouldn't I feel that way? His actions are speaking a lot louder than his words.

Despite the fact that he's not a sports nut, an over-indulging drinker or a "hang out all night with the boys" type of guy, his recent decision has destroyed what little respect I had left for him. He has plunged himself into a car restoration project that has put our marriage at the edge of a cliff, overlooking an endless abyss of misery.

Although we're deeply engulfed in debt, he borrowed $400.00 from a friend to buy a 1965 Pontiac Bonneville. The *hunk of junk needs so much work! It doesn't even run! He had to have it towed to our house. "How are we going to afford this?" I ask him. He tells me not to worry; he'll do all of the work himself and he'll get any parts cheap because the car is so old.*

So far, this entire ordeal has been a nightmare! I cried the day that car arrived here and it seems as though I've been crying every day since. I guess one would ask why am I being so difficult about something that seems so harmless. But they don't know how it feels to be second to a big old piece of crap in the driveway! Before he began this project, my husband promised that he'd buy me the wedding ring that he couldn't afford when we got married almost six years ago. He promised to turn our upcoming anniversary into a special wedding event where we could renew our vows. I asked him last night, with tears in my eyes, "How is any of that going to happen when you've already spent a month using any extra money we have buying parts?" I told him that he spends all of his free time in the garage and that we barely spend any time together anymore! He promised that everything would happen as we planned and that he would cut back on working on the car as soon as he's fixed the all-important fuel line. Then he could get it running. The conversation ended with me saying, "Yeah, whatever!" He was too tired from the numerous activities of the day to argue the matter further.

My conflict was compounded by my visit from Manny. He showed up out of nowhere earlier today, shortly after my husband left for work. It was as if he sensed my pain and came to heal me. As always, he was a welcomed breath of fresh air. He's still a great listener and comforter. I was able to unload my anguish on his waiting solace. True to form, Manny was prepared to relieve my anxiety. He lovingly reminded me of the first time the two of us became one. We fondly reminisced about those days of love and discovery. Soon our deep memories set aflame our most intense passion for one another. We made love again for the first time in years. Our interlude left me with a multitude of ravaging emotions. On the one hand, I felt guilt for having betrayed my husband and our marriage. On the other hand, I felt entitled to love, compassion, attention and sensitivity. All of which was provided by Manny. I felt alive whenever his fingertips touched my skin. However, I felt saddened after his departure, knowing that a day with my husband didn't compare to a brief moment with Manny.

Again, my thoughts of Manny are replacing those of my husband. However, it has been a great relief to think of something other than how neglected and unwanted I feel. Unfortunately, not all of my thoughts surrounding Manny are good ones. Since he left this afternoon, my reflection has shifted toward the time when our dance was over and I was left in the middle of a lonely floor....

Chapter 14

The Dance Ends

The following weeks were spent in a blissful utopia of being in love and making love. The best aspect of our relationship was the bond of friendship that we created. Throughout hours of telephone conversations, we were never at a loss for words. We never experienced "awkward silence." Yet, when we were together, there were times when silence was all that was needed. We would lay in each other's arms just listening to the whisper of every breath.

Once Manny confided, "I'm never at peace unless I'm with you."

He was a tortured soul. I wasn't aware of all the details, but from everything I had been told and had seen, I knew he was suffering inside. Whenever he arrived at my house, I could see a wave of relief rush over his face.

I found myself feeling more like his wife than his girlfriend. I *wanted* to take care of him and soothe him. I *needed* to be the one that he turned to for refuge.

He hated going home. Often, he would leave work and come straight to my house. I'd even have dinner waiting for him. He'd shower, and afterward, we'd share a dance of love and lust. I felt as though we were newlyweds; every day was a honeymoon.

Gradually, problems became apparent. Manny would make plans with me and then wouldn't show up or call. I would be beside myself with worry.

That's not like him at all! He'd never stand me up, he isn't like that! I said to myself.

{"Maybe he is now."} I hadn't heard from that voice in weeks.

So that meant there was trouble.

At first when he would disappear, I would worry, but progressively, my fear turned into anger. More and more, he was breaking dates and not being home when I called. When he'd finally call to explain why he hadn't shown up as planned, the pieces just didn't fit. All of this was just too familiar to me. I was petrified that he would do exactly what all the others did. The signs all pointed to his inevitable departure.

To make things worse, I received an unexpected visit from someone I thought I'd never see again—Malcolm!

One day, I was waiting for Manny to show up when there was a knock at the door.

Finally! I thought. *Manny's here!*

I sprang to the door and flung it open only to find Malcolm standing on my porch.

"Hi, Olivia. Can I come in?"

I stood in the doorway, bewildered. I was curious as to what he could have possibly wanted. However, I was also concerned that Manny would show up during Malcolm's visit and then there would be bloodshed. Manny could be very territorial. His temper had a hair trigger, and even though he told me I could never do anything to set him off, I was aware of the kind of things that did. High on the list of things that brought out that side of Manny: ex-boyfriends and other guys that didn't appear to respect his relationship. So I had to get rid of Malcolm as quickly as possible.

"Hi, Malcolm. What are you doing here?"

"I had to see you. Please, Olivia can I come in?"

"This isn't a good time. Could you come back tomorrow?"

"Why? Is *he* here?"

"Who?"

"Your new boyfriend. You know, the guy you dumped me for."

"Wait a minute, I didn't break up with you because of another guy, you know why we—"

"I'll only be a few minutes, please." His voice was labored.

"Okay, just a few minutes."

Malcolm walked by me and into my living room. He didn't sit. I walked over to him and then he grabbed me. He hugged me tightly and said, "I still love you."

"Where is this coming from, Malcolm? You had your chance to prove that you loved me and you said you needed time. But, *I just didn't have time* for your games."

"I was in a car accident a few days ago."

"What? Are you hurt?"

"No, but I got a pretty bad scare. The car was wrecked, but no one was injured."

"What happened?"

"I didn't come here to talk about that. Honestly, I came here to tell you that I've changed. Even before the accident I missed you and thought about calling you. But afterward, I knew I had to tell you how I feel. You just never know if you're going to be around another day to tell the people you love just how much you love them."

I was stunned. Malcolm was gentle and appeared very genuine.

"Olivia, I don't expect you to leave him and come back to me, but if you ever need me, I want you to know that I want to be there for you. I gave up too easily and I let you give up on us. If I had another opportunity I'd jump at it. But if I could at least be your friend, I'd jump at that too."

"Thank you, Malcolm. I'm glad that you want to be friends. I didn't think we could get passed our break-up. I didn't think you cared about me at all, especially during the last few weeks of our relationship."

"I never should have made you feel that way. I'm sorry."

I hadn't seen that side of Malcolm since we first started dating.

Before I knew it, he was leaning in toward me. He pulled me close and then—**KNOCK! KNOCK!** We were both startled by the sound. I jumped out of his arms and almost out of my skin! I knew Manny was right outside that door.

{"How are you going to get out of this one?"} That voice was taunting me.

That's all I needed! I had to do something.

"Don't worry, Olivia, I'm leaving. But you'll be hearing from me, because I want you back."

I couldn't believe he dropped a bomb like that on the way out the door, as my boyfriend stood, waiting to come in!

"Wait, I thought you just said you wanted to be friends."

"I want you, Olivia, anyway I can get you. But I'm not giving up on us just yet."

He unlocked the door and pulled it open. While waving goodbye, I said, "Well, nice seeing you again. Take care."

Instantly I noticed the look on Manny's face, but fortunately, Malcolm walked by him without an altercation. Malcolm said, "Hello," and Manny responded with a "What's up, man?" Neither of them said another word to each other. Manny stepped inside.

"So, where have you been?" I asked nervously.

"Oh, no—first tell me what Malcolm was doing here."

"How did you know that was Malcolm? You've never met him before!"

"Who else could it be? If I were him and I lost the best thing that ever happened to me, I'd show up trying to get you back. Isn't that what he was doing?"

"Well…yes…and no. He said he wanted me back, but that he would be content with a friendship. I really didn't have much time to respond, but I told him I wouldn't mind being friends with him."

"He won't settle for a friendship, Olivia."

"Why wouldn't he?"

"Because I wouldn't."

"Well, he's not you. And you're not him."

"Is there a chance that he can have more than a friendship with you?"

"Why? Are you jealous?" I taunted him. "I mean, you can't seem to show up on time for our dates and you've been missing in action lately. Why should you care?"

He wasn't amused. His eyes were fixed on me; seconds seem to pass like hours. And then before I knew it we were kissing ravenously. We ended up tearing through our clothes, doing so without saying a word. Soon we were on the floor deeply engrossed in a scorching throng of pleasure.

Finally, Manny spoke, "You're mine, Olivia. I won't let you forget that."

As his thrashing got harder and faster, his words got stronger, as he repeated, "You're mine! You're mine! You're mine!"

I loved every second of it! I wasn't afraid of Manny. I could never think he would hurt me, physically. He wasn't abusive, not even possessive. He only ***said*** the things that ***I was feeling*** and ***thinking***. ***I was his and I would never leave him.***

Again, the time came for us to part. We didn't speak another word about Malcolm the rest of the evening. But later something disturbing occurred.

Manny called me when he got home and he didn't sound like himself. Before I could ask him what was wrong, someone was beeping in on call waiting.

"Hold on, Manny."

"Hello?"

"Olivia, it's Malcolm."

"Malcolm? What's going on?"

"I need to talk to you."

"I can't, I'm on the phone with Manny."

"Okay, I'll call you back." Abruptly, he hung up.

"Manny, are you there?"

"Yeah. Who was it?"

"Um, Malcolm, but he didn't want anything."

"Of course he wants something—you."

"Sweetie, you don't have to worry about that at all."

For the first time ever, Manny's vulnerability seemed to surface. Throughout our numerous conversations, his sensitivity was always apparent, but usually he still had an air of confidence. That night, he sounded unsure and insecure.

"I'm not going to leave you, Manny. You know it's over with Malcolm."

"I'm sorry that I haven't been able to come over very much lately.

I hate it when we're apart. I can't wait to leave this house and live on my own. I want you to come with me. I want you to move in with me."

"What? I—"

KNOCK! KNOCK!

"Hold on, someone's at the door."

I looked out the window and whom do I see?

"Malcolm!" I opened the door. "What are you doing here?"

"I had to talk to you."

"Hold on, stay here. I'll be right back."

"Wait, can I come in?"

"Oh, yeah, okay, come in and shut the door behind you."

"Um, Manny, can I call you back?"

"Who's there Olivia? Is it Malcolm?"

"Well, yeah, but I didn't know he was coming over. I'm going to get rid of him and I'll call you right back. I promise."

"Okay. I'll talk to you later." Manny sounded cold.

Damn! I thought. *What is going on?*

"Olivia."

"Malcolm, what are you doing here? It's a good thing my mom is working late."

"I had to see you again. I didn't get to finish talking to you today."

"What is it that you didn't say before?"

"This." Swiftly, he moved in and kissed me.

I pulled away. "What are you doing?"

"I know you still love me, Olivia, and I'm not going to let you forget it."

"I can't believe this. I can't do this with you. I'm with Manny."

Malcolm turned to leave. "That's fine, Olivia, I just wanted to let you know how I feel. Don't worry. I'm not going to pressure you. I know you're with Manny, but I doubt if he'll be around much longer. After everything you've told me about him, he'll break your heart soon enough."

"I wish you wouldn't say those things. Manny has changed."

Obviously unconvinced, he said, "It's late. I'd better get going.

I'll see you later." Malcolm walked out the door after kissing me on the cheek and flashing a smile.

I ran to the phone and called Manny. No one answered. I called again, still no answer.

Where could he be? I wondered.

I began to get undressed and ready for bed and then I heard... **KNOCK! KNOCK!**

"Who in the world would be here this late? God, I hope my mother doesn't walk into this mess!"

Looking out, I saw Manny standing on the porch. I opened the door and smiled.

"What are you doing back so soon?"

He came in and walked me over to the couch.

"Olivia, what did Malcolm want?"

"You came all the way over here because of Malcolm! How did you get here anyway?"

"I got a ride from my friends. They're outside waiting for me. So, what did he want?"

"He wanted to reiterate that he still loves me. But that doesn't matter, you know that!"

Manny's hand began to tremble. I'd never seen that side of him.

"Olivia, you know I love you, even if I can't always be here with you."

I covered his shaking hand with mine and then whispered, "As long as you want me—and even if you don't—I'll be yours, forever."

I really think that I reassured him. He gently kissed me on his way out and told me that he loved me. I was elated! I couldn't believe that I had two guys that wanted me! But actually, I was ecstatic that Manny felt threatened. The situation revealed how deeply he needed me. I was glad to know that we truly had a connection and Manny didn't want to lose that.

After that night, I didn't see Manny for a few days; I barely even spoke to him. He wasn't home most of the time and he didn't return my phone calls. One day, he showed up unannounced. Although I was glad to see him, I was also angered by his nonchalant, "here one minute, gone the next" attitude.

{"I thought he didn't want to lose you. I thought he needed you."} That voice cut through me like a blade!

An argument erupted between us. Manny's excuses just didn't satisfy my suspicions and I made that abundantly clear.

"Why is it that just a few days ago you were visibly shaken by the mere thought of another guy taking your place, but now you have no problem with the distance that's been building between us?"

"I can't talk about this anymore. I have to get going. I'm sorry." Manny's reply was unusually unfeeling.

"Why are you doing this to me?" The tears were building in my eyes.

"Don't worry, I'll call you later, I promise." And then he was gone.

That night he finally revealed what he didn't have the courage to say in person. I answered the phone, only to hear, "Olivia, I'm not mad at you, I just need some space."

I became catatonic. The tears poured from my eyes. I didn't speak.

"I'm sorry, but I'm going to stay with my brother in St. Clair Shores. It's not that far from here, just outside of Detroit, but I just won't be able to see you for a while."

"Why? If you're not going to be that far, why do we have to stop seeing each other?"

"I can't explain, I just—"

Anger evoked my words. *"Oh, of course you* ***can't explain****! Or maybe you just* ***won't explain****!* ***You never do!*** *And I just sit back and patiently wait for you to trust me enough to tell me the truth! Damn you, Manny! What do you want from me? Do you expect me to sit around* ***AGAIN!*** *And wait for you to figure out whatever it is that's keeping you from me?! Do you expect me to wait for you forever?!"*

"I don't expect you to wait forever. Olivia, I don't want to hurt you."

"I've heard you say that before! You never ***want*** *to hurt me,* ***you just do****! I can't believe this is happening! Why do you keep running away from me?"*

"It's not like that! I love you, I just can't be with you right now."

"*And I don't get any further explanation than that! I don't get anything, right? You're leaving; you don't know when you'll be back, so take care, see you when I see you! I thought I meant more to you than that!*"

"You do, but I just can't give you anything else. I can't tell you anything more than I already have. I'm really sorry and I—"

I began shaking violently and crying uncontrollably. At that moment, something inside of me shattered.

"I HATE YOU!" I screamed as loud as I could. *"I HATE YOU!"*

I threw the phone against the wall and held myself as I wailed.

"I hate you, Manny," I whispered. "I hate you. I… I… *I... love you.*"

I lay curled in a ball and cried for what seemed like an eternity. Throughout my suffering, I realized that it was over.

"It's finally over. Our dance has ended and the music has stopped. Here I am left on the floor all alone... ***Here I am...alone again****."*

Chapter 15

The Journal—Part Four

Dear Journal,

I've been crying for hours. My husband is at work and I haven't heard from Manny all day—even though I've been thinking of him. I couldn't help but to remember when he walked out of my life for the second time. I was happier than I'd ever been in my entire life and in one instant it was over. The fact that I'd never been happier made my suffering even more severe. During that time, I cried endlessly, I couldn't eat and I could barely sleep. On the rare occasions when I did fall asleep, I was haunted by dreams of Manny. When I closed my eyes, I could see him, and every time he was running away and I couldn't catch him. Sometimes the dream would change and I'd get a chance to talk to him briefly. I'd beg him to stay, but he wouldn't respond, he'd just turn and walk away. I would scream and beg, but he wouldn't turn around or answer.

That following year was hard. However, Malcolm was true to his word: "if you ever need me…I'll be there for you." Shortly after picking myself up off the floor, I remembered him saying, "After everything you've told me about him, he'll break your heart soon enough." I didn't call him because I didn't want to hear him say "I told you so."

I didn't speak to anyone. I didn't make or receive any calls. I went to school in a fog and I worked in a daze. No matter how many people asked me what was wrong, I couldn't bring myself to say that I had been dumped again.

One day, Malcolm showed up suddenly. He told me that he'd been calling, but I hadn't been answering the phone and I wasn't returning any of his messages. I finally broke down and revealed my shame. I admitted that Manny had left and that I knew he was never coming back. Ironically, he didn't judge me or criticize. He didn't gloat about his words coming true. Malcolm comforted me with kind words and a listening ear. Gradually, a friendship blossomed. I wasn't looking for a relationship and I knew I had no right to turn to Malcolm after breaking up with him in the beginning. Yet, during those next several months, he rescued me from my grief. I'm not sure how or when it happened, but one day, we became a couple again. Malcolm was always honest about his feelings for me. Despite my deep feelings for Manny, Malcolm wouldn't give up on us. Maybe I just wanted to be loved or maybe I just wanted to forget. At first he was my comforter and then my friend, eventually, he became my lover again.

We shared a year of good times, Malcolm and I. Of course, we weren't anything like Manny and me, but we were stable and that was a pleasant change of pace. We went out to the movies, out to dinner, out to visit friends and family. We were good together...for a while anyway.

At the end of that year, the day came when I saw him—Manny was back. He was riding down the street on his Helix and I couldn't believe my eyes. Then a couple of weeks later, there he was walking through the mall. Again, I was able to see him without him seeing me. I hadn't thought of him in several months; even my dreams had stopped. I was over him, so why did I care if I ever saw him again? I began to think that I had imagined those sightings.

Finally, I ran into him on the way out of an eatery and I turned away and bolted! I began to hyperventilate and felt faint. That's when the dreams started again. Every night, I could see his face when I closed my eyes. It became worse than before; the images were more vivid and realistic. I was being tormented again!

I couldn't tell Malcolm because I'd made a promise that Manny was out of my system. I promised him that his love had healed me and that I didn't want or need the chaos Manny brought to my life. I promised that our upcoming anniversary would be the mark of our future. I promised that I'd never hurt him again. I promised...so many things. I couldn't tell him about Manny. The twisted madness that overcame me was something I had to endure—alone.

I became determined to confront my fears and battle my lunacy. My resolve was unwavering, I wasn't going to let Manny destroy my life again, especially when he didn't even know he was doing it!

Without Malcolm's knowledge, I made it my number one priority to purge Manny from my soul. Who knew that undertaking would result in the darkness being lifted and the dawn breaking through the clouds...?

Chapter 16

The Darkness & the Dawn

"Manny! Manny! No, please don't go! Manny! Wait!"

I awoke trembling and chilled by a cold sweat.

Not again! Damn him! This is the second week in a row that I've been dreaming about him! Why is this happening again?

{"You know why."} That voice always knew when I was in trouble.

I do know why. It's because after a year, I've started seeing him everywhere!

I couldn't believe it. I'd finally moved on with Malcolm and we were looking forward to our first anniversary. Neither of us had stayed in a relationship that long. Only a couple of months to go and we could both celebrate proudly. We were good for each other. We were happy together, so why did it matter if I ran into Manny or not? Why did seeing him again send me into a downward spiral through anger, pain and nightmares?

"Why am I being tortured again?" I whispered through quiet tears. "I can't live like this! But how I do let go of this pain?"

{"Maybe you should say good-bye to it!"}

I thought that was dumb! How could I say good-bye to my pain? If it were that easy, I would be cured by now, right?

And then it hit me! I never really said good-bye to Manny. In fact, both times he walked out of my life I didn't have my say. I didn't have a chance to fully express my emotions and by doing so, fully closing the door on our relationship.

That's it! ***I need closure!*** *Maybe if I didn't have these unresolved* *feelings, then I could truly move on with Malcolm and not look back!*

So I decided to do the unthinkable. *I'm going to call Manny.*

{"Are you sure about that?"} *Yes, I know now that I have to call him. Once and for all, I'm going to tell Manny how I feel and walk out of his life. That's the only way to stop these dreams and to really be free of him. I'm not going to let him hurt me anymore. I have to get him out of my system for good!*

The next day was spent in a cloud of suffering. Although I was sure that calling Manny was the only way to be released from that prison of unresolved emotions, I didn't think I'd have enough nerve to actually do it.

{"Olivia, you've had too much nerve at times! I know you can do *this*!"}

"That was odd. Why would that voice be rooting for me now?"

It didn't matter why. I knew it was right! I had to face him.

So after school, after work and ultimately right before bed, I finally gathered all of my courage. I retired to my room, closed the door and sat on floor next to the phone. For a moment, I sat there listening to the soft music I had playing in the background. I took a deep breath and picked up the receiver. Quickly, I dialed Manny's number. The ringing seemed ten octaves higher than normal. Then suddenly, I heard, "Hello?"

I opened my mouth to respond, but only my breath escaped. I was unable to utter a sound.

"Hello?"

It was him. Manny was at his house—not in St. Clair Shores—and on the other end of the line.

"Hello? Whoever this is, say something or I'm hanging up!"

Still, I was mute.

"Fine." **CLICK!**

Tears began to stream down my cheeks. I began to sob.

What am I doing? Why am I such a loser?

{"You aren't a loser!"}

Yeah right! Why was Manny even at his house if he was supposed to be out of town?

{"So what! He was there and that's good because you're able to do what needs to be done. Call him back and put an end to your suffering! You're stronger than you think! Show Manny what a mistake he made giving you up!"}

I wiped my face and thought in response, *That's right! I've come a long way and I'm not going to shrink into a ball of spinelessness! I'm tired of allowing guys the opportunity to cut me down and walk out of my life without even hearing a word of opposition! I've got to do this!*

An hour had passed until I was fully prepared to make the call. Finally, I was ready. Dialing the phone that time was less dramatic. I was more determined the second time around.

The ringing was normal again, but it didn't last as long. Before I knew it, I heard, "Hello?"

Once again, Manny answered.

"Hi, can I speak to Manny?" I kept my voice light and confident.

"Speaking." I was surprised he didn't say more. I thought he would have recognized my voice, but why would he? It had been a long time.

"Do you know who this is?"

"Yes." Again, he offered nothing more than a one-word reply.

Although I was slightly shaken by his tone of voice and his lack of conversation, I was still on a mission.

"I don't believe you. I don't think you have a clue as to who I am."

"Honestly, I think I know who you are, but if you are who I think you are, then I must be dreaming."

That answer was unexpected.

"What do you mean by that?"

"You sound like someone I've wanted to talk to for so long, but I thought I'd never hear from again."

"Why wouldn't you hear from that person? What did you do to them?"

"I hurt them very badly and I regret it deeply."

I was hoping that he was referring to me, but I couldn't be sure. I didn't think he'd leave me again, so how could I be certain that during his absence he hadn't gotten involved with someone else and hurt her just the same. How could I be sure he wasn't mistaking me for his new girlfriend? How could I know?

"Oh, well if you regret it so much why didn't you call them to apologize?"

"I couldn't. I didn't want to hurt her again."

"How would apologizing hurt this person?"

"For her, I would have had to do more than apologize and I wasn't in any position to give her what she needed or deserved."

We had come full circle; we began with riddles and mind games and that's where we had ended up again. I realized that I was being pulled back into Manny's hurricane of intense energy and magnetism. I had to get to the point.

"Well, I didn't call to hear your tale of woe. I don't care if you know who I am or not at this point. But you're going to hear me out. You'll figure it out by the time I'm through." I was firm and convincing. "We used to know each other, you and I. When our relationship ended, I didn't handle it very well. I'm sure you've probably heard this before. It's obvious, that you're the 'love 'em and leave 'em' type. Anyway, without your knowledge, I couldn't sleep for weeks and I barely ate. When I finally began to fall asleep at night, I was tortured by dreams of your continuously walking out of my life. I cried for months and my self worth was disintegrated. After months of that misery, I was finally able to pick up the pieces of my life and move on with someone else."

Manny had been silent until that moment and then he interrupted. "So if you've moved on, then why are you calling?"

{"He sounds almost wounded and jealous."}

I thought I detected the same, but I couldn't be sure so I continued.

"That's simple. Recently, I've been seeing you all over town and for some reason my nightmares have started up again."

"Oh, really. Well, what does your boyfriend think?"

"He doesn't know, but that doesn't matter. Listen, I don't expect or want your sympathy, and I know you couldn't care less."

"Well, if that's how you feel, then why are you telling me all of this?"

"Because I need to say it and you need to hear it! You walked out of my life without looking back and I didn't get a chance to tell you how I really felt. Now that I've had time to get over you, it's time to tell you where you can get off!"

"Olivia, I'm surprised at you! I never thought you'd ever talk to me that way."

"So you figured it out."

"I knew it was you the second I heard your voice."

"Yeah, right. If you recognized my voice when I first called, then you would have said something."

"I did."

I knew what he meant. I thought he was trying to open up the waves of subliminal communication, but I just wasn't sure at the onset.

"Well, it doesn't matter if you figured out who I am. The fact is, I've only told you a quarter of the pain I've been dealing with. I can't believe that after everything we shared you could walk out on me and not look back. There's no telling how long you've been back from St. Clair Shores and you didn't even bother calling me!"

"I couldn't! I mean that I planned to call you in just a few months. I came back for you."

"How dare you lie to me like that?" Fury began to build. "I'm not falling for that again! You weren't going to call me! Why would you? You got what you wanted and then you had no further use for me, so why would you bother to call me, especially after another year! I can't believe I ever loved you! I can't believe I ever believed anything you ever told me!"

"You believed me because you loved me and you still do."

"I'm not going to do this! Malcolm and I are going to celebrate our one year anniversary in a few weeks and I'm not going to let you ruin my life again!" I shouted.

"Oh, so you went back with Malcolm. I thought you would."

"Don't even try it! It wasn't like I was waiting to get you out of the picture so Malcolm and I could be together. He was a friend to me when I thought I couldn't trust anyone. He was a friend to me when I thought I was too worthless for anyone to care about me. Eventually, we just ended up together and—"

"And Malcolm got what he came for that night—you."

"Why should you care? You didn't want me!"

"I wanted you more than I wanted my own life! Don't ever think that I didn't want you! I'll never stop wanting you!"

"Whatever! If you wanted me, you would have stayed with me because I was already yours."

"You're right, you were mine! And you still are!"

"What? Didn't you hear me? I've gone on with my life! Malcolm and I are happy together; there's no way I'm falling for you again!"

"You already have! If you didn't still want me, you wouldn't be dreaming about me and thinking about me and calling me to *try* to get me out of your head!"

I couldn't believe he could be so cruel.

"Is this a game to you? Does stabbing me in the heart thrill you so much that whenever you get a chance to do it, you go for it? How could I have been so wrong about you? Maybe I did love you, but now I can see that I never should have wasted my time!" I was cold.

"Please, wait, Olivia. I'm so sorry. I shouldn't have said that. I'm so glad you called because I can finally give you all of the things you deserve. I can finally tell you the truth. We can finally be together!"

"You have to be kidding! I'm never going to trust you again, Manny! And I won't ever leave Malcolm just to get hurt by you again. Not to mention the fact that I don't believe you ever had any intentions of coming for me. ***I called you,*** remember!"

"I need you to give me your new phone number."

"What? How do you know we have a new phone number?"

"Because I know you moved in with your mother's new husband and didn't keep the old one. I also know you still go to the same high school and you work down the street from there. I know everything about you, Olivia, because I never really let you go. So give me the number."

"Why should I?"

"Because you're wrong about me and I want to prove it! I know you and Malcolm are together. I don't want to disturb that."

"I'm leaving in less than five months. I'm going to be moving to Lansing to go to Michigan State University. So don't bother wasting your time on some new mind game. I won't be around long enough for you to watch me suffer."

"Well, if you're leaving town and you're solid with Malcolm, then there's nothing wrong with giving me your number. I'm not trying to disrupt your life or your plans. I want to show you that I'm sorry for the way I've treated you in the past. Please, just let me spend these last few months trying to make up for all the hurt I've caused you. Listen: write down my pager number. When you're ready, you can put your number in and I'll call you back. No pressure."

"Why should I call you at all?"

"Because you know you have nothing to lose."

After thinking about it briefly, I felt confident enough to take his pager number.

I'll never have to use it. I reasoned to myself. *I'm not going to let him think I'm not strong enough to resist temptation.*

After writing down the number, we ended our conversation.

For days after, I felt strong and free. Even my dreams stopped. I finally felt like I had closure.

I don't have to worry about Manuel Nelson ever again.

{"Are you sure about that?"}

Of course, he's out of my system for good.

{"Are you just stating a fact or trying to convince yourself the statement is a fact?"}

That's crazy! My dreams have stopped. I'm finally free.

A week passed and I found myself looking at that pager number lying on my desk.

I wonder what he's doing. I wonder if anything he said last week was true. I wonder if he really was going to come for me. I wonder….

{"I knew it."}

Knew what?

{"You still love him."}

Maybe so, but it doesn't matter. I'm with Malcolm and I know I can never trust Manny again. The answer is obvious.

{"Page him. Take whatever you can get until you leave."}

That voice was never a champion for "Manny and Olivia," but I was quite relieved to hear it concede.

I didn't waste time. Before I knew it, I was dialing the phone. After the message I put in my number and hung up. I sat on the bed.

What have I done? Manny's going to destroy me all over again.

{"Only if you allow him to."}

Moments later, my phone rang.

"Hello?"

"Hello, did you page me?"

"Manny, it's Olivia."

"Hi, Olivia. I didn't recognize your number, but I recognized your voice as soon as I heard it. I'm glad you called."

That phone call launched the renewal of our friendship. During the following two weeks, the present paralleled the past. Manny and I talked almost every night. I didn't realize it until then, but I really missed confiding in him. Manny was always a wonderful listener and friend. We caught up on the previous events of the passed year. It was as if no time at all had gone by. Manny could always make me feel as though I was the most important person in his life—whenever I was able to stay in it long enough.

During the recovery of my friendship with Manny, I never revealed what was happening to Malcolm. I didn't want to hurt him. I honestly thought that Manny and I could be friends. However, it didn't take long for me to discover Manny's true intentions.

Shortly after our late-night conversations began, Manny and I met at the mall. It was the first time we rendezvoused since before our break-up. I was glad we were in a public place. As usual, upon laying my eyes on him, I was completely swept away. I knew I had to maintain my composure for several reasons. First of all, Manny and I were only friends and I was determined to keep it that way. Secondly, I was still involved with Malcolm and I couldn't allow myself to be pulled back into Manny's black hole of passion and electricity. I couldn't hurt Malcolm the way Manny hurt me.

What kind of person would that make me? I thought as I walked up to Manny.

We engaged in small talk, but Manny's attitude was strangely boorish. Soon our discussion got heated. Manny began to insist that I was capable of cheating on Malcolm—even leaving him again. He made it quite clear that friendship with me was no longer an option, flexing his "possessive" muscles.

"Your love for me will force you to either cheat on him or leave him entirely."

"Where is this coming from? Why are you saying these things to me?"

"I came back for you, Olivia. I need you to understand and come back to me."

"You actually think my love for you will be strong enough to make me hurt the one person that helped me to get over you? That's funny, because my love wasn't strong enough to keep you from hurting me, now was it?"

"Is that your only reason for not giving me this last chance? All you've said is that you don't want to hurt Malcolm, but you haven't said that you don't want me. If Malcolm wasn't in the picture, would you give me the chance then?"

"Well…maybe… I don't know! But it doesn't matter, because ***he is*** in the picture! He's my future and we're happy together! **I don't need this right now!**"

"**No, *you just need me*!**"

"I'm leaving."

"Alright, but you're only hurting Malcolm by staying with him."

"What? That's the dumbest thing I've ever heard!"

"Why? It's the truth. As long as you stay with Malcolm, you'll always wonder what we could have been together. You'll always compare him to me and he'll never stack up."

"That's it! Stay away from me, Manny! I guess it's my turn to walk out on you."

I turned and walked away, hearing behind me, "Olivia, this time would have been different, I swear!"

I left him standing in the middle of a crowded mall, looking like a jilted idiot. That thought alone made me smile to myself. I headed home feeling empowered and in control.

"I turned my back on Manny the way he'd always done to me. If that's not closure, then I don't know what is!" I whispered haughtily.

The following weeks were so hectic that I didn't even think about Manny—or maybe I just didn't want to believe that I was. At any rate, there were so many last-minute preparations to make for graduation and my move to Lansing. I had already been to my prom with Malcolm a couple of week's prior, but my big anniversary dinner was approaching. Everything was falling into place. I was graduating—the third out of my class. I was happily involved with a very nice guy and I was on my way out of my mother's house on to my own life in college. I even got the satisfaction of closing the door on Manny—slamming it in his face, to be exact! I was flying high and I didn't think anything could change that.

When graduation day arrived, I was confident and unnerved. I was even prepared to give the small speech I was assigned, introducing the keynote speaker. I was elated that day. I walked across the stage and accepted my diploma with honor and pride. However, I began to realize that a part of me looked for Manny's face among the crowd.

Could he be here? He said he'd always find me, could he be here watching me graduate? I began to ponder.

{"The real question is: would you like him to be here?"}

I didn't have time for another debate. My thoughts were quickly interrupted by the activities of the day and by Malcolm.

"Hey, beautiful! You looked great out there!"

I hugged and kissed him. After the ceremony, Malcolm took me home to celebrate.

That stupid voice was wrong. I didn't want Manny at the

graduation, because I had Malcolm. I didn't need anyone else.

Before I knew it, my one-year anniversary with Malcolm had arrived. Although we'd been planning for that day for two months, nothing could have prepared us for what happened that night.

Chapter 17

Hoover

After everything I'd been through during the passed several months, I was thankful that I made it to my anniversary night. Malcolm and I had made reservations at a nice restaurant that neither of us had ever been to before. I even had my mother's permission to extend my curfew until midnight. All of our plans were on track.

When the evening arrived, I was content. I felt certain that I made the right decision concerning Manny. I was also sure that I deserved that night with Malcolm. As I made the last-minute adjustments to my hair and wardrobe, I thought, *This is it, my night to remember!*

This was the first anniversary I'd ever been able to share with anyone. I was finally able to experience stability and security within a relationship that didn't drag me down. I was finally happy.

{"Are you?"}

Oh, don't you start, because I—

The doorbell rang.

"Malcolm's here!" I shrieked.

After a last-minute check of the new dress I'd bought for the occasion, I scurried to answer the door. Smiling, I flung it open.

"Hi, Malcolm...." My voice trailed away when I saw him standing there.

{"What is he wearing?"}

"Um, I feel a little overly dressed... I...."

I couldn't believe Malcolm was standing in front of me wearing black jeans and a casual shirt. I was sure he would have put forth more effort for what I thought was our special night.

"You look great, Olivia. Are you ready?"

In a fog, I grabbed my purse and walked out the door.

{"Olivia, let it go."}

I began thinking that maybe I was being overly sensitive.

What's the big deal about his attire? It's nothing. That's just the way Malcolm is, I privately rationalized.

The drive to the restaurant was the second disappointment of the night. We got lost and argued most of the way. I became so angry that I could no longer hold in my disgust.

"Malcolm, what is your problem? I thought this was a special night for you and me? Look at you! You're dressed like you're going to a house party down the street or something!"

"Oh, so now you don't like the way I dress!"

"That's not it. I just thought you'd put forth more effort for our anniversary night!"

There was a brief silence. Suddenly, Malcolm said, "I'm sorry, I guess you're right. Let's just get to the restaurant. I don't want to fight anymore. I don't want to ruin our evening any more than it's already been ruined."

I tried to understand, "Okay, that sounds good to me."

Those words were the last spoken until our arrival at the restaurant. When we entered and were seated, I finally felt more at ease. Cheerfully, we ordered our meal. The tension had faded, so I turned to Malcolm warmly.

"I'm glad we're here, sweetheart. I'm glad we made it to this place in our lives."

"Yeah, it's great."

{"Is that all?"}

I was suddenly propelled into a thought-provoking dilemma, *Why doesn't he seem more excited?*

{"Maybe because he isn't!"}

No, no, everything's fine. I'm just being melodramatic, I thought.

"Olivia, are you okay?"

"Yes, Malcolm, I'm sorry. I started to get lost in my thoughts, but I really wanted to tell you something."

"Alright, go ahead."

"Well, I just wanted to thank you for helping me through this passed year. I wanted to tell you that your love helped me when nothing else could. I wanted to tell you that I'm finally over Manny and I—"

"Wait a minute, what do you mean you're ***finally*** over him? I thought he was out of your life last year."

"He was… I mean he ***is*** out of my life, I just wanted to use this opportunity to reassure you that—"

"Why would I need to be reassured?"

"Malcolm, don't get defensive. I'm honestly thanking you for loving me and supporting me. I'm trying to tell you that I love you and could have never gotten over the pain Manny caused me without you."

My explanation seemed to calm Malcolm, but secretly, it unnerved me. Throughout the evening, I was plagued by disquieting feelings. In fact, I became so overwhelmed with uneasiness that I barely made it through the night. I ended up telling Malcolm that I came down with a headache and would have to cut our date short.

"I'm sorry things didn't go as smoothly as I thought it would, Olivia. I hope you feel better."

"I will tomorrow. I just need to get home and rest—too much excitement, I guess."

Relief swept over me like an ocean wave when I walked through the door of my house. I greeted my mom and then ran to my room.

What's wrong with me? Why was tonight such a disaster? Why did I even bring up Manny's name?

{"I think it's time you faced what you've been running from."}

What am I running from?

{"Manny."}

No, that's over.

{"After tonight, how can you believe that? Maybe he was right."}

Manny wasn't right about anything.

{"You *were* comparing Malcolm with Manny tonight! When you saw how Malcolm was dressed, the first thing you thought of was that Manny wouldn't have showed up dressed like that if ***you two*** were celebrating your anniversary. And then when Malcolm seemed less than enthusiastic in response to your sweet words, you thought of Manny again!"}

I don't remember thinking any of that!

{"You're in denial! Maybe you should listen to your subconscious more often!"}

I can't believe—

The phone ringing disrupted that argument.

"Hello?"

"Olivia."

It was Manny.

"Manny?"

"Yes, it's me."

"I thought you got the point a few weeks ago. I won't let you hurt me anymore."

"I'm not calling to hurt you. I need to tell you everything that I've been keeping from you for two years. I need to tell you what's been keeping us apart."

"That sounds interesting. You're finally going to come clean! I'm all ears! Let's hear it."

"I don't want to tell you over the phone. I need you to come to my new place."

"Oh, you have a new place?" I was surprised to hear that.

"Yes. Olivia, I finally moved out of my parents' house forever! I'd been saving money for months. When you called me, I was still living at home, but I was only a couple of months away from moving out. Now I'm living on my own and I can give you everything I've always wanted to give you. Can you come over so we can talk?"

"I don't know about that. Where did you move to anyway?" I wanted to keep the conversation light.

"I live down the street from your school and your job—on Hoover."

"You moved to a place right down the street from my job? Why?"

"I know you probably don't believe me, but it was a coincidence."

"Well, I still don't think it's a good idea."

"Why not? I just need to talk to you in person. I can't tell you everything that I want to over the phone."

{"You know you want to."}

"No! I'm not coming over there, Manny. I can't. I told you that I'm with Malcolm. We don't have anything to talk about."

"Please, Olivia. I'm only asking you to come over once. After I explain why I *had to* push you away so many times, you'll see that I haven't been playing games with you. I *need* to see you, please."

"I'm sorry, Manny, I can't come to see you. If you can't tell me over the phone then send a letter, a telegram or a message tied to a pigeon! I'm not coming to see you."

I could hear the disappointment in his voice, but still he persisted. "Can you please think about it? This could change both of our lives. Write down my new phone number and if you change your mind call me."

I was silent, using that moment to contemplate my next move.

"Alright, I'll take the number, but I'm not coming over there." I was determined to keep Manny at arm's length.

Happily, Manny spouted off the phone number to his first apartment. I could hear the jubilation in his voice. I'd never heard him sound so light-hearted and excited.

"I've got to go now, Manny, I'll talk to you later."

I hung up before he could respond.

Briefly, I looked at the phone number in my hand and decided to get rid of it.

Manny's hurt me enough! I've got to let him go!

I ran to the kitchen and grabbed the matches. Quickly, I struck the match and lit the paper on fire. As the phone number burned in the kitchen sink, it was being burned into my memory. After walking away from the ashes, I could the see the numbers in front of my eyes.

How did that happen? I only looked at it for a minute! No one could memorize a phone number that fast!

{"Of course someone could. Especially if she was desperate to hold on to it!"}

If I were so desperate to hold on to that number, I wouldn't have burned it!

{"Wake up, Olivia! This is your chance. Don't blow it! All this time you've wondered why Manny kept running away. And now you have a chance to find out what the mystery has been, let him tell you. You deserve to know."}

What good will it do? I'm Malcolm's girlfriend, remember?

{"But you want Manny, and maybe this time you can actually have him!"}

Reflecting on the events of the evening sent me on a journey through memories, emotions and desires. Thoughts of Manny swirled around my head.

Loving him is all I've ever wanted to do. Loving him is all ***I want to do****.*

I thought I could get over Manny, but the truth was, I could never get over a love so intense that it was unsurpassed by that of any other.

I've ached for Manny since the first day I saw him. Maybe I should start being honest with myself. I've never gotten over Manùel Nelson and maybe I never will.

{"So, the least you could do is hear him out."}

I smiled. At last, the gravity of the situation became apparent, so much so that it almost knocked me over!

Manny wants me! He's got his own place and he wants to talk to me in person! Am I crazy?! I have to see him! I've been waiting for this forever!

I ran to the phone and dialed the number etched in my head.

"Hello?"

"Manny."

"Olivia." The relief in his voice jumped out at me.

"Okay, I'll come—but just to hear you out." I didn't want to appear overly anxious.

"Can you come tomorrow afternoon? I'll be home from work by 4 p.m."

I agreed to the time. Manny lived less than two blocks from my job, so getting there by 4 p.m. would be a breeze.

He gave me his address and said, "Thank you, Olivia."

That was it. Manny simply thanked me and hung up, but the tone of his voice said more than his actual words. I could hear the joy he felt at just the thought of my visit.

Before going to sleep, I whispered to myself, "I can't believe I'm going to see Manny tomorrow at his own place on ***Hoover*** Street. I can't wait."

Ironically, I didn't think of Malcolm or our anniversary the remainder of the night. The next day was no different. All I could think of was Manny. I narrowly made it through the day. When I was at the point of feeling as though my head might explode, I realized that the time had finally arrived.

Hurriedly, I punched the clock and ran to the parking lot. I was no longer thinking rationally. I was running on pure adrenaline and instinct. All I could think of was Manny, and all I wanted was to see him.

During the brief drive down the road, I reached a startling conclusion: "**I can't stop *loving*** him. **I can't stop *wanting*** him. And **I can't stop *needing*** him. **I can't stop**…."

Before I was aware of it, I was pulling into his driveway. I took a deep breath and turned to leave the car. I looked up and there he was standing in the doorway, waiting for me. We smiled at each other. I managed to walk up the path to where Manny was standing. Seeing him always made me feel like I was losing control of all my senses.

"Olivia, I'm so glad you made it, come in."

"Hi, Manny," I said nervously.

{"Pull yourself together and get down to business."}

That was much easier said than done. As soon as I entered Manny's new home, I felt transported back to the day when I first visited his room at his parents' house. Although his apartment wasn't as elaborately decorated, I felt as if I was entering Manny's private universe.

Manny kindly took me on a tour, proudly gushing over every

inch of the place. Soon we were back in the living room on the couch.

"Olivia, I don't know where to begin."

While avoiding eye contact with him, I replied, "Just start at the beginning."

"Well…Why won't you look at me, Olivia?"

"I can't."

He brushed his hand across my cheek and then turned my face in his direction.

"I know why you can't look at me."

"I didn't come here to play games, I came to hear what you have to say." I was desperately trying to be strong.

"Alright, that's fair. But when I'm done, I'm going to make sure you never take your eyes off me again."

I hated when he talked like that, because I was sure his words would come true, with or without my consent.

"Olivia, I couldn't stand leaving you, but I never should have come into your life in the first place." Manny paused briefly, as if he were searching for just the right words. "Remember when I told you that my father didn't like me hanging out with black people?"

I nodded in response.

"Well, I also told you that my father wasn't saying very much about me seeing you, but I lied about that."

"What was he saying?"

"He was doing more than just *telling* me he didn't want me to see you."

"What do you mean?"

"I mean that my father and I were getting into some very heated arguments and physical battles over you."

"What?"

"From the beginning, I knew my mother and father wouldn't stand for me dating black girls. But I wanted you…I *needed* you so much. I tried so hard to fight loving you. That's why when we first met; I was so distant and cold to you. No matter how mean or cruel I was to you, you would *still* look at me as if I was the only person in the whole world for you. I couldn't figure it out! It was like you knew I was hiding my real feelings, even though there was no way for you to have known anything about me. I started to think you could see something in me that no one else could and you hadn't really spoken to me yet. At that point, we hadn't had a chance to get to know each other, so I was confused by your stares and shy smiles. Slowly, I was being stripped of my guard." He stopped. I could see through his eyes that he was reliving every memory.

"At first, I was trying to discover what you were all about. Most girls were either afraid of me or wanted to use me as some kind of trophy to show around town. But the more I got to know you the more I realized that *you didn't want anything* from me. All you wanted was for me to let you in. I couldn't believe it! You were the most special and beautiful girl I'd ever met."

As he spoke, I could feel myself being drawn in...closer and closer. Like the power of gravity, the power of Manny was unmistakable. *Who was I to fight the pull?* I secretly thought.

I continued listening intently to his confession.

"I won't lie, I've had opportunities to be with all kinds of women, some prettier, some older, some more sophisticated than others, but none like you. When you realized I wasn't just going to rip down my walls for you, you patiently waited for me to trust you. You accepted whatever I had to offer, but you always gave more than I deserved."

His expressions brought tears to my eyes. Each word affirmed my belief that Manny truly loved me.

"I guess my feelings for you made me forget the situation I was in—for awhile anyway. That's why I asked you to break up with Josh so that you could be mine, but the day before you came over, my father and I had a huge fight about my friend Nate. He called him every nasty, racist name he could think of and then I realized I couldn't bring you into that. The next day, I pushed you away—"

"I remember that. I was crushed when you did a complete 180 and said we could be friends, but nothing more."

"You might have been crushed, but you were still so persistent and determined. I only ended up getting back with my ex-girlfriend to turn you away for good...and to settle things down at home. She wasn't black; she was a nationality that was more tolerable to my parents." He dropped his head as he spoke, "I hated myself for hurting you, but I didn't know what else to do."

"I can't believe that you were going through that! So, why did you come back the last time, if you knew your dad was going to attack you over dating me?"

"Because I couldn't stay away. The entire year was spent missing you. I left that girl a couple of months after I stopped talking to you. I didn't love her. I couldn't find in any girl what I found in you. I ended up in agony over you. I started not to care what my father thought. I was fighting with him over everything and getting kicked out of the house every other month anyway. I figured, why not have the only woman I've ever loved by my side? What did I have to lose? That's when I called you. We ended up having the most intense and wonderful relationship I'd ever experienced."

"Yeah, it was wonderful, but then you left—again with no real explanation—supposedly to move to St. Clair Shores. So what happened?"

"Things got worse than ever. I tried to hide my relationship with you. But while I was trying to hide you from my parents, I was also trying to hide that whole situation from you. I didn't want you to know what was happening. I remembered what you told me about that guy Josh and his racist mother. There was no way you'd let anyone suffer for caring about you, so I didn't want you to blame yourself and break up with me. At first, I thought I could do it. I was juggling lie after lie, telling my father different stories about where I'd been when I was really with you. There were times when I couldn't make it over to see you because my father would start a fight with me and keep me in the house. Then I had to lie to you about where I was."

"Why didn't you tell me the truth? I asked you if I was causing you any trouble!"

"I loved you and I thought I could handle things. Besides, it was more than that. I ended up going to St. Clair Shores, but only for a little while, after my father and I had a fistfight."

"Oh my God! I can't believe you got into a physical fight with your own father over me!"

"He'd pushed me around before, but nothing like this. When you met him that one and only time in my living room, I tried to make up a cover story. I told him that you were Nate's girlfriend and we had just been hanging out, but since you were calling me for weeks, it was easy for him to figure out that I was lying. Everything exploded one day when my father confronted me. I tried to stand up to him, but he punched me in the chest, knocking me off of my feet. And then he threatened me. He told me that he'd rather kill me than see me dating some 'nigger.' "

Manny's eyes were blank, as if he could see back in time, watching his father stand over him with clenched fists.

"Why couldn't you tell me this before? It wasn't your fault! I would have backed off, I wouldn't have called, I wouldn't have given you so much grief about missing dates with me...I...."

"I was ashamed, Olivia."

After hearing those words, the picture was so clear and it showed all over his face.

"Ashamed of what?"

"You thought so much of me, you felt things for me that no one ever did. I was afraid that if I told you what was going on at my house, you'd think less of me. I was afraid that you'd wonder why I didn't stand up and fight my dad, why did I let him get away with keeping us apart! I wondered that myself, so why wouldn't you?"

"Because despite the fact that you are the most passionate and head strong person I've ever known, you still had to live under your father's rules; I could never think less of you for that!"

"I wanted to believe that, but I didn't want to get hurt. I thought if you found out, you'd not only lose that sparkle in your eyes when you looked at me, but that you'd walk away. I couldn't take it ***if you rejected me***—you mattered to me so much. It was easier to walk away from you, but not that much easier."

I sat listening in awe.

"Recently, when I saw you running away from the restaurant I was coming out of, our eyes met just for a second, and I could see the pain I'd caused you all over your face. I wanted to run after you, but it wasn't time yet. Even though I had been planning my 'escape' for months, I wasn't free at that moment."

"Your escape?"

"Yeah, I went back home the last time with a plan to make sure I'd never have to go back there ever again. Since I stopped going to school, I could work as many hours as I wanted. Every paycheck I got, I saved. I didn't buy anything for months! I was getting ready to move into my own place. When you called six weeks ago, I was surprised to hear from you. I didn't think I'd ever hear from you again. I was already determined to move out of my parents' house and come looking for you, but after talking to you, I became even more determined to reach my goal. I just wasn't ready yet. I had enough money saved, but I was still looking for a place to stay—that took more time than I expected. Your call changed everything for me. I sat listening to you reveal how you'd been dreaming about me and missing me. I knew you were still mine. Your love for me was rare and precious, a perfect reflection of you! Even though you were dating Malcolm, ***you never stopped loving me***. That was an unexpected treat."

"What was an unexpected treat?"

"The fact that you loved me so much, you actually tried to forget about me by going back to your ex-boyfriend! But no matter what you did, you never forgot about me, just like I never forgot about you."

The more Manny spoke, the more exhausted he seemed. Slowly, a weight was being lifted from his soul.

"I was so afraid that by the time I was able to come back for you, you wouldn't love me anymore."

"Since I never admitted that I still loved you how could you be sure that I did?"

"The same way you were sure that there was something inside of me worth finding. Olivia, I just knew. You and I have a connection that goes deeper than just a sexual attraction. You can hear me calling to you, even when I haven't said a word. And I can hear you whispering to me, even when we're not in the same room."

Manny's words had never been so profound. He always spoke eloquently, but I'd never heard him describe our bond so flawlessly.

He continued, "I never should have insulted you the way I did at the mall. I was getting frustrated. I had been holding this in for so long and the closer I got to you the more I wanted to take you away and tell you everything. But, I didn't want to tell you anything until I was set up in my own place, that way I'd never have to hurt you again; I'd never have to leave. So when you walked out on me, a torch was lit under my feet. I looked even harder for an apartment and even got Nate to be my roommate."

"Nate is your roommate?"

"Yep. Even though I had all of the money for the security deposit and the last month's rent, I wanted to make sure that I wouldn't have a problem keeping this place. So I invited my buddy, Nate, to stay and split everything fifty-fifty. That way, I'd never have to go back to that prison, I called home! A couple of weeks after I moved in here, I called you."

"Why did you wait a couple of weeks?"

"Because I was scared."

"Scared of what?"

"I thought that after you left me in that mall, you were done with me. I thought that I'd finally lost you for good. I couldn't get the picture of you walking away from me out of my head. I knew I had been a big jerk. That's why it took me that long to build up the nerve to call you."

Tears crept to the surface. It was the first time I'd ever seen any man unveil such fragility.

"I can't lose you, Olivia, not after everything I've been through to be with you."

I was speechless.

He pulled me close to him and began kissing me softly. I lost myself in his arms. I missed his kisses so much. His touch was undeniably the most exhilarating I'd ever felt. Each fingertip contained an immeasurable amount of unlawful voltage! No one should have been allowed to have that much power, but Manny possessed it naturally.

Our gentle kisses turned into an insatiable hunger for more. We simultaneously began to grab at each other's clothes.

"I've dreamt of making love to you again, Olivia," he said almost breathlessly.

His words, although beautiful, brought me out of the cloud of lust I was experiencing. I pulled away.

"I can't, Manny. I can't."

"Why? I know you love me. I've explained everything. What more is there to talk about?"

"Malcolm! Remember him! I can't cheat on him or hurt him. I know you explained everything and I believe you, but maybe you're too late. Besides, I'm moving to Lansing in just a few months. What are you going to do then?"

"I know you still want me—more than ever! And just because you don't want to hurt Malcolm you're going to give up on us, when this time there's nothing standing in our way. I didn't let my father keep us apart forever, so what makes you think I'm going to let your guilt about Malcolm keep us apart? And if I have to, I'll follow you to Lansing, because I've already wasted too much time! I'm not going to let anyone or anything come between us again. You know that we belong together. You can't turn your back on me and live with yourself, not now that you know the truth. "

I knew Manny was reading my thoughts, reciting what I felt word for word. Before I could respond, he grabbed me and began kissing me wildly. I couldn't resist the onslaught of emotions that followed. I was enthralled! The more his hands touched me, the more I didn't want him to stop. This time our clothes were removed completely. We ended up on the floor tangled intensely in each other's arms. After kissing what seemed to be every inch of my body, Manny abruptly pulled me on top of him. The moment of union was so ravenously arousing that a geyser erupted between my legs. With each movement, I was aware of Manny's every thought. With every motion, our bond was reinforced. Making love with Manny was as natural and as unavoidable as the changing seasons. No matter how we feel about it, winter changes into spring, spring into summer and so on. Likewise, no matter how much I thought I should fight it, Manny and I were an absolute inevitability.

As always, Manny's stamina was steadfast, allowing me an unlimited amount of pleasure. For some unexplainable reason, reality struck. *Malcolm!* I screamed in my head. Suddenly I remembered Manny's words: "Your love for me will force you to either cheat on him or leave him entirely." As confusion began to rock me like an earthquake, tears poured down my face.

"No!" I screamed, pushing Manny away.

"What's wrong?"

Sobbing, I collected my scattered clothing and ran to the bathroom to dress.

"I can't do this, Manny! I've never cheated on anyone before in my life! I can't believe that I ended up doing exactly what you said I would!"

"Don't worry, this isn't a fling! We love each other! We need each other! Please don't leave like this!"

As he fought to convince me to stay, I tore out of the bathroom, dressed and heading for the door. Manny grabbed my arm.

"Please don't go. Let's talk about this! Don't leave things this way!"

Through tears of shame, I responded, "I can't hurt anyone the way you hurt me! I understand why you did it, but I just can't see myself destroying someone's life the way you destroyed mine! I have to go!"

Manny's tears resurfaced. He hugged me tightly. "Please, Olivia, I need you! Don't leave."

We were both crying as I exited and ran toward the car. I didn't look back at him; I couldn't believe how close we were to finally being together. I peeled rubber out of the driveway, unsure of what to do next.

"I love you, Manny!" I whispered. "So what do I do now?"

Chapter 18

The Decision

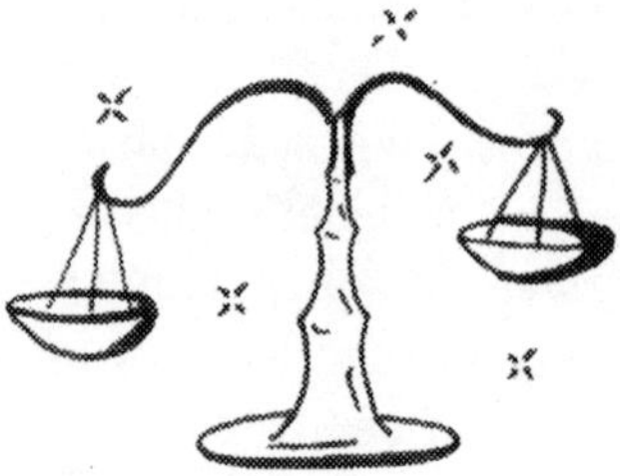

By the time I made it down the road, I was crying uncontrollably, so I pulled over.

{"Calm down, girl! You've got to think things through."}

I had no idea Manny was going to affect me that way. I didn't know that we were going to end up making love. I should have realized it; Manny always did have a way of turning me inside out.

Several minutes passed, I wiped my face and gathered my thoughts. *I have to see Malcolm. I have to sort things out.*

{"Are you sure that's a good idea? Maybe you should just go home and talk to Malcolm later."}

No, I can have with Malcolm what I have with Manny, can't I?

{"Don't fool yourself. You already know that nothing compares to what you and Manny share."}

I gained my composure and started for Malcolm's house.

I pulled into his driveway and walked up to the door. I trembled as I rang the doorbell.

The door opened, Malcolm stood in front of me smiling.

"Hi, sweetie. What a surprise! Come in."

I was so racked with guilt that I felt nauseous.

"What's wrong? You look like a stiff wind would blow you over."

I hesitated briefly. "I had to come, Malcolm. There's something we need to talk about."

"Alright, but come here and give me a hug first."

Malcolm squeezed me tightly and kissed my lips gently. I was so uncomfortable that I pulled away.

"What is it, Olivia?"

"It's Manny."

Surprisingly, Malcolm's gentle tone was swiftly doused with anger.

"Manny again? I thought you were finished with him! I'm tired of this, Olivia! I've tried to make you forget that loser, why do you keep talking about him, especially now after all of this time?"

"Because I've heard from him."

"What? You've talked to Manny! What did he want?"

"Well, he wanted to explain why he had to leave—"

"Why ***he had to*** leave! Sounds like you've already heard him out and taken pity on him! Is that it?" Malcolm walked up to me and grabbed me by the arms. "Is that it?"

I'd never felt threatened by Malcolm or any other man, but at that moment, fear flooded my heart.

Pulling away, I said, "I've talked to him."

"You haven't seen him have you?"

I could no longer trust Malcolm's reaction to my words, so I decided to say, "No, of course not. But I did talk to him over the phone. That's why I'm here. Talking to Manny and hearing his reasons for leaving has confused me. If everything he told me is true, then you and I shouldn't have ended up together. I mean…he wouldn't have left me if he didn't have to and now I can't help but to wonder what could have been."

Malcolm's face was turning red. His voice heightened. "I spent months listening to you whine and cry over this fool! And now he comes back after a year and gives you some sob story that you eat up with no questions asked! So what does that mean? You don't love me?"

"Malcolm, I do love you. That's why I came here. I need you to help me sort this out."

"All you ever did was ***use*** me to forget him. No matter what I did I was being compared to ***HIM***!" Resentment was apparent in his voice.

"That's not true! How was I supposed to know Manny was going to come back? Why are you treating me like a criminal all of a sudden?"

"Because I know that Manny is the only person who can come between us. I've trusted you since we met, you've never given me a reason not to, but Manny is your weakness. I'm not going to walk through limbo like before. I'm giving you one week. If you come back here a week from today, Friday afternoon, then I'll know that I'm the one you want. If you don't show up here, I'll know Manny is your choice. After the decision has been made, there's no turning back. If you choose me, I don't want to hear another word about Manny, and you can never see or talk to him again. If you choose Manny, you'll never see or hear from me again."

I was shocked that Malcolm could pose this ultimatum to me, but I was relieved that I'd have more time to think.

As I turned to leave, I responded, "Fine, my final decision will be made by the end of the week."

Then I left to go home.

I don't know what caused it, but by the start of the week, I was very ill. Perhaps my extreme emotional state weakened my immune system. Whatever the reason, I came down with a stomach flu that kept me in bed for days. Although I didn't have to worry about missing school, since I'd already graduated, I still felt bad about missing work.

For two days, I lay in bed thinking of the decision I had to make. On the second day, I was so overwrought by the thoughts rolling like thunder in my head that I felt even more ill.

I wanted to confide in someone. I needed to talk to a friend. I had a best girlfriend, but I didn't feel compelled to share this with her. I needed to talk to the one person who knew me best.

"Hello?"

"Manny, it's Olivia."

"Olivia, Hi! How are you?"

"I'm stuck in bed with the stomach flu. I feel terrible."

"I'm coming over, I need to see you."

"No. I look awful and I don't want you to catch what I've got.

Just stay on the phone and talk to me. Please."

His voice was soft and comforting. "Alright."

"I've missed you," spilled from my lips.

"After the way you left here a couple of days ago, I wasn't sure that I'd ever hear your voice again."

"Why didn't you call me?" I was afraid of his answer.

"I don't know. I thought you'd be out with Malcolm, ***deluding yourself***!"

"What's that supposed to mean?"

"I was only giving you time to realize what you know is the undeniable truth—we belong together. And you're delusional if you think staying with Malcolm is the answer. But I've waited this long, I can wait a little longer. I know you'll come."

Hearing Manny's voice soothed me. I confessed my dilemma.

"After I left your house, I went to see Malcolm. I was going to confess what we did, but I couldn't."

"Why not?"

"Because I was afraid. I've never felt threatened like that by Malcolm before, but when I told him that I heard from you, it was like he snapped or something."

"What? Did he hurt you? I'll kill him!"

I'd never heard Manny sound so defensive on my behalf.

"No, no, he grabbed my arms, but he didn't hurt me. I just felt uneasy, so I decided not to tell him what happened between us."

"Well…what did you tell him?"

"I told him that you called to explain everything and that it wasn't your fault that you had to leave. He didn't like the fact that I believed you and forgave you."

"So what did he say?"

"He gave me an ultimatum. He told me that I have until Friday to decide who I want to be with—for good. He said that if I choose him, I can't speak *to* you or *of* you again. However, if I choose you, I'll never hear from him again."

"That's going to be the easiest decision you've ever made."

I chuckled at his obvious haughtiness.

"Oh, and what makes you say that?"

"At first, when you left my house crying, I thought that you'd never come back, but once I had a chance to think, I came to a conclusion."

"And what is that?"

"You can't stop loving me. You can't stop wanting me and you can't stop needing me. You can't stop…Just like I can't stop."

I was astounded at how he knew my thoughts. That's exactly what I was thinking while I was driving to his house the other day.

But how did he know that? I secretly wondered.

"Since you're such a genuinely good person, your conscience is bothering you. Honestly, if you didn't feel bad about what we did while you're still Malcolm's girlfriend, then you wouldn't be the girl I love. Everything that you are keeps me coming back to you, but until you let go of your guilt, those will be the same things keeping us apart."

At that instant, the decision was made. No matter how I felt about Malcolm, it was obvious that he didn't know me as completely as Manny did.

{"It's about time you've accepted the truth."}

"Manny, why are you being so nice to me when I could decide not to hurt Malcolm and stay with him?"

"Because I know you and you *can't* stay with him—especially not after everything that's happened between us."

Words from his lips were thoughts from my heart. No one could see inside me the way Manny could.

KNOCK! KNOCK!

"Olivia, you have a visitor," my mom yelled.

"Manny, can I call you back? Someone's here to see me."

"Okay, I'll be waiting."

I dragged myself out of bed and put on my robe. I went to the living room, only to find Malcolm sitting on the couch.

"Hi."

"Malcolm, what are you doing here?"

Pulling flowers from behind his back, he said, "I'm here to see how you're feeling. I called your office yesterday and they told me that you were home sick. The girl at the front desk thought you'd be out for a few days. I just wanted to tell you that I'm sorry about what happened the other day."

I didn't know what to say.

"Um, Malcolm, I know that I have a decision to make and—"

"Don't worry, I'm not pressuring you. You still have until Friday, but I know you'll be at my house. After the way Manny hurt you, I know you'll never trust him again. I'm just giving you the time you need to come to the right decision."

Before I could say anything, Malcolm kissed me on the cheek and quickly exited. I stood there bewildered for a moment. Then I took the flowers he'd given me and put them in water. My first thought was to call Manny and that's exactly what I did. We ended up talking into the wee hours of the night.

The next day was no different. After he got home from work, Manny called me. We ended up on the phone all evening laughing, sharing stories and making up for lost time. Our friendship was as solid as our love. My decision was final. I wanted a life with Manny, no matter what I had to do. Consequently, I planned to make my decision known in just two days.

By Thursday, I was well enough to go back to work. I think everyone noticed the difference in my demeanor, because many asked me why it looked as if I were glowing. Inside, I was beaming with excitement and joy. I couldn't wait to begin my new life with Manny. I decided to wait until Friday to let both Malcolm and Manny know. I didn't want Malcolm to think that I rushed into deciding our future. And I wanted to make Manny sweat it out a little.

While sitting at the front desk, answering the phones, I was shocked to see who appeared before me.

"Malcolm! What are you doing here at my job?"

Quickly, he pulled another bouquet of flowers from behind his back.

"I came to see you. I miss you so much, I just wanted to let you know that I'm always thinking about you."

"Well, I wish I could talk, Malcolm, but I've got to answer the switchboard."

"That's okay, I just wanted to drop off the flowers."

"Cheaper than having them delivered," I said with a smile.

"No, that's not it. I was dying to see you."

A pang of guilt stabbed me through the chest.

"I'll let you get back to work, Olivia. I love you and I'll see you tomorrow."

Before I could speak, Malcolm was gone. I didn't even have time to absorb what had just happened. The phones were ringing off the hook. However, after work the intensity of the situation had a chance to sink in.

Tomorrow, I'm going to devastate Malcolm.

{"But you're also going to make Manny the happiest person on earth."}

Does that matter? How can I hurt someone who's been so good to me?

{"The truth is, you are hurting Malcolm, no matter what decision you make. Manny has said it and Malcolm has sensed it. You compare them. You try to pick Malcolm apart in hopes that something inside of him will be what you really want. How is that not hurting him? Breaking up with him is going to be difficult for both of you. But don't you think that staying with him and trying to make him fit into someone else's mold is going to destroy him?"}

I sat in my room meditating. I realized that regardless of what happened between Manny and me, Malcolm and I had no future together. I wasn't happy about having to break Malcolm's heart, but I was overjoyed with the thought of making a fresh start with the only man I'd ever really loved.

The next day was one of reckoning. Surprisingly, I was at peace with my decision and myself. As the time drew near, I became more anxious to bring the matter to its conclusion. I was aware that all I had to do in order to make my resolution known was to show up at either Malcolm's or Manny's. So after leaving work, I drove to the only place where I knew my future would lie.

After pulling into the driveway, I was overwhelmed by a sense of exhilaration and elation. I exited the car and ***ran*** to the porch. I noticed that the door was already open. Inside I found Manny waiting for me, wearing only a towel.

"Hi."

"Hello, Olivia. I knew you'd come."

I could feel my cheeks beginning to glow red. "What's up with the towel?"

"I just got out of the shower. I didn't want to miss watching you pull into the driveway, so I rushed out to open the door and wait for you."

"How did you know I was coming here, Manny?"

"Because I know you."

Manny stood up and walked over toward me. He brushed against me gently. His hair was damp and flowing across his shoulders. I thought he was going to take me into his arms, but instead he moved past me, closed and then locked the door. My heart was pounding. I had no idea what he was going to do next. He walked around me and then grabbed my hand, leading me into his bedroom.

Upon entering, Manny closed the door and turned to speak. "I knew you'd come to me, Olivia," he whispered.

"You would know, wouldn't you?" I replied.

Our mouths were then drawn together like two powerful magnets. As we kissed, Manny undressed me. Moments later, his towel dropped to the floor; we followed thereafter. Passionately, yet tenderly, Manny made me aware of how much he had longed for that moment.

"Finally," he whispered, "*finally*."

It was as if he were filled with ecstasy, as well as a sense of relief. Manny seemed absolutely intoxicated with me. Afternoon turned into evening. Our time together painfully drew to a close. Whenever Manny and I had to part, it felt as though we were being surgically removed from each other and no anesthetic was being used. Manny kept trying to get me to stay with him. He wanted me to spend the night.

"I can't, Manny, my mother would kill me."

"I hate being away from you."

"I know, but I'll be back tomorrow."

We kissed each other gently as I exited. I smiled at Manny as I drove away.

When I got home there were several messages on the answering machine. Suddenly, I remembered Malcolm.

I hope this isn't him on the machine.

I quickly played the messages.

"Olivia, how could you do this to me? I thought you loved me? Do you think you're going to get away with this? It's not over yet…**CLICK!**"

Oh no! Malcolm didn't accept things as well as I'd hoped.

{"That's an understatement."}

The next message was from my mother.

"Olivia, call me when you get home. I'm still at work. Malcolm called here looking for you earlier and when I told him that you weren't here, he showed up anyway, asking where you were. I told him that you were with a friend, but he didn't seem too happy. Is everything all right? Call me."

He went to my mother's job looking for me!

I quickly called my mother and calmed her fears. I told her that I was fine and reminded her of the decision I made. I had previously confided in her about the ultimatum I was given. The night before, I told her that I had chosen Manny and would have to break up with Malcolm.

"I know. That's why I was worried. Some guys don't take rejection well."

"Don't worry, Mom. I'm home safe. The doors are locked and no one's getting in here."

"I'll be home in about an hour."

"Okay, Mom, see you soon."

I went back to checking the messages. The third message revealed that Malcolm had been drinking. His words were slurred and I could barely make out some of the things he was saying. The phone rang before I could hear the rest of the messages.

"Hello?"

"Olivia, are you okay?"

I was so relieved to hear Manny's voice. I explained what had been happening. I conveyed to him that Malcolm didn't sound as if he were taking things well.

"I thought he said that he'd accept it; no matter who you chose, the decision was final."

"I guess that's when he thought I'd choose him."

Call waiting began to ring.

"Hold on, Manny. Someone's on the other line. Hello?"

"Olivia, how could you do this to me?" Malcolm's voice was sad and his words were garbled.

"Malcolm, why are you doing this? You said you'd accept whatever decision I made."

"We've been together for a year! I helped you when that punk left you! And now you're leaving me for him—again!"

"I'm so sorry, Malcolm. I never should have let things go this far between us. I thought I could get over him. I really tried. I just didn't think Manny would ever come back. I truly didn't mean to hurt you."

"I should come over there right now and show you what pain is!"

"Are you threatening me?"

Before he could answer, I could hear his mother in the background calling me terrible names.

"I guess you told your mom about all of this."

"Yeah, what did you think I'd do? She really liked you; she had a right to know that you weren't ever coming back."

"Have you both been drinking? She sounds just as bad as you do."

"Yeah, we've both had a few drinks. So what! You're not my girlfriend anymore, why should you care?"

"Why don't we talk tomorrow, Malcolm, after you've sobered up."

"Why, is *he* there?"

"No, I just need to talk to you when you're not so upset. I have to go. I'll talk to you tomorrow."

Quickly, I clicked back over to Manny.

"I'm sorry, that was Malcolm. He had been drinking and his mother was in the background calling me names and…."

"Calm down, Olivia. What else did he say?"

"He said he wanted to come over here and show me what pain really was. You don't think he'll come, do you?"

"No, he'll pass out and sleep it off. But if you want me to, I can come over."

"Well, my mother said she was on her way home. If she comes home and finds you here, things might get ugly. I'll just keep the doors locked."

"That's good. Don't open the door for anyone, especially Malcolm."

Manny and I talked for a little while. As usual, he comforted me, making me feel as though we were the only two people left on the planet. We ended our conversation after making plans to see each other the next day.

"Before you go, Olivia, I want to tell you something."

"Yes."

"I never thought I could be this happy. I've been miserable most of my life, but you changed all of that. You made me believe that someone could love me unconditionally. You made me *believe in love*. Thank you."

I responded by saying, "I love you so much. The words don't hold enough meaning to describe just how much."

That night, I went to sleep feeling as though my life was headed in a new, exciting direction. The summer was only the beginning of the adventure, soon I'd be off on my own, moving to Lansing.

But what happens to Manny and me then?

Chapter 19

The Journal—Part Five

Dear Journal,

I've recently discovered that coming face to face with your past can devastate the present, as well as the future. This journey that I've been taking through my history with Manny has led me down so many pathways. Most of which have been filled with love and passion, but too many that have been plagued with pain and uncertainty.

Each time he's come back into my life, I've received him—this time was no exception. To me, Manny is like an overpowering addiction. I believe this is so, not just because being with him sends me soaring on an immeasurable high, but also because whenever I'm tempted with his presence, I'm unable to resist.

We've been spending many intense moments together, retracing our steps. I admitted to him that loving him has always been at great cost to me. He didn't think that was a fair assessment. So I took him back to the time when I was being tortured by dreams and needed to gain absolute closure. I relived how loving him has brought me to my emotional knees, time after time. However, he responded by reminding me of the reason he had to leave and what leaving me did to him.

I rebuked him by revisiting the time when I was put in the terrible position of "choosing between him and a guy who was innocently in the path of the Manny Tornado!"

He laughed at my analogy. His response was, "You made

the only choice you could have—you chose true love."

When he talks like that, I honestly have no defense. I have to wonder how my marriage will fare under such overwhelming attacks of forbidden desire and longing.

My marriage: what marriage? I feel alone when Manny isn't here. That's why I accept visits from him. I need him and he knows it.

My husband and I haven't seen eye to eye on anything during this previous year. He's always busy with work or an automotive project. When he is home, he's either tired or horny! There doesn't seem to be any room for a more detailed spectrum of emotion. He wants affection, he wants sexual satisfaction, but I want consideration and passion.

Often, all my husband talks about is what he wants to do next to that hunk of junk in the driveway. If restoring that Bonneville is all he talks about, I'm sure that's all he thinks about as well. It's as if my needs are of no concern. So far, there's been no renewal of our vows and no wedding ring. Actually, I can't remember the last time my husband bought me something as a gesture of love and appreciation. I often feel that he doesn't notice me at all. So how can he appreciate what he doesn't realize he has?

On the other hand, Manny is always concerned with my needs and my feelings. Whenever he and I can steal moments together, the world we share is exclusive and exotic. He's attentive and romantic. I'm his number one priority. Loving me seems to be what powers his existence. The hold he has over my life is profound. It's as if we are forever bonded—no matter where we are or what happens between us.

As I stated earlier, loving Manny is an addiction. It's powerful, it's dangerous and it's satisfying, all at the same time! So why is it that I'm not married to him? How did I end up here, having an affair, instead of being happily involved with the only man I've ever loved? But most importantly, why, if Manny keeps leaving me, won't he just release me?

I suppose many of the answers can be found by examining the events surrounding my move to Lansing. From there, my life with Manny was irreversibly altered—forever. The most wonderful summer I'd ever spent was followed by the most horrible year of my life. It all fell apart…in Lansing.

Chapter 20

Lansing

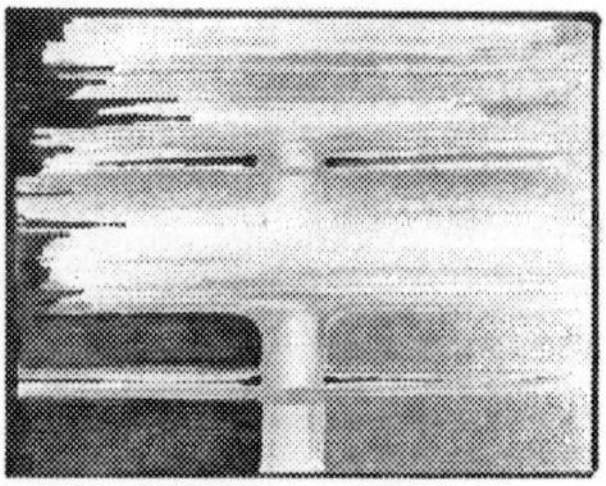

My decision to give Manny another chance came with a great price. I broke the heart of an innocent, loving young man whose only shortcoming was that *he wasn't Manny*. I hated hurting someone who'd given himself to me as a shield from pain. At the very least, I needed to attempt to make Malcolm understand that he was trying to combat something stronger and more powerful than the force of wind.

The day after I disclosed my choice by going to Manny's house instead of Malcolm's, I received a call from the scorned party. Although grieved by the events that unfolded, Malcolm was sober and ready to listen. In fact, he insisted on coming over to hear me out. I thought I owed that to him. Despite having plans with Manny later in the afternoon, I allowed Malcolm to stop by for what I hoped would be an absolution for both of us.

Upon his arrival, Malcolm was surprisingly pleasant, positive even.

"Hi, Olivia," he said after gently kissing me on the cheek. "Can I come in?"

"Sure, let's sit down so we can talk."

In silence, we walked over to the couch. Finally, Malcolm spoke.

"I'm not letting you go this easily."

"What?"

"I thought about it and I'm sure now that I didn't handle things right. I never should have forced you to choose like that. I didn't even give you enough time to really think about our relationship. I know we can work this out…."

"Malcolm, please don't."

"Don't what?" he asked while moving closer to me, and then taking my hand. "I know you're not just going to throw away what we have just like that."

Slowly I wiggled away from his grasp.

"Malcolm, I wanted to take this time to tell you how sorry I am and to explain some things to you."

{"I think he's in denial,"} that little voice whispered from afar.

"Listen, I never wanted to hurt you. The year that we spent together was very special to me, just as you are and always will be. I don't want you to think that I have no feelings about you or what we shared. The fact is, I care about you deeply and that's why I can't stay with you."

"That doesn't make any sense, Olivia! You love me, and I love you, that's all there is to it."

"No, there's much more to it than that. I do love you, Malcolm, but I love Manny with all that I am. I'm not saying this to hurt you, but the truth is, Manny is in my blood! Somehow he became a part of who I am, and I can't break free from him. I guess it's because I really don't want to."

"You don't want to? Why? He's hurt you so much, why don't you want to get rid of this guy?"

"Because I sincerely believe that Manny left me against his will. I know that his family is prejudiced toward African-Americans. His father strong-armed him into staying away from all black girls, especially me! I can't blame him for that."

"But you can blame him for not telling you the truth in the first place."

"That's true, I *could* blame him, but *I don't*. And even if I did have problems with the fact that Manny hid the entire truth from me, it doesn't change the way I feel about him. I need you to understand that I've made a commitment. I'm going to see this through. I'm going to take this ride with Manny wherever it leads me. This is an opportunity that I can't walk away from. Unfortunately, you got caught in the middle of all of this. I can't tell you how sorry I am about that. But if I stay with you now, I'll always wonder what I could have had with the man that's defined what love is for me. Now I can see what love is so clearly. It's not trying to change someone or settle for someone else. Manny has taught me that the meaning of love centers on trusting your instincts. No matter how much he pushed me away, I sensed his true feelings for me. When I was oblivious to the details of his miserable childhood and family life, I could feel his pain from across the room. I questioned my own logic, but in the end, I was right. Manny loves me and I'm not going to give up on that."

"You actually believe all of that? You think that he loves you? I'm the one who loves you!"

"Malcolm, I've tried to explain my actions and emotions. If you don't want to accept what I've said, that's fine, but that just means you're going to leave here believing there's still a chance for us, and there isn't. So all I'm asking is that you go and don't look back. I hope all of this will sink in and you'll be able to move on with someone else without holding on to the past."

"If you want me to leave, then give me one last kiss, or I'll stick around until *he* shows up."

"Why do you think Manny is coming?"

"Because if I had the chance to be with you again, like he does, I'd rush over every day of the week. I'm sure he's on his way."

Malcolm had guessed right. Manny was on his way shortly, and since talking to Malcolm took longer than expected, I was afraid the two of them would run into each other.

"Why are you doing this? Giving you a kiss won't do any good."

"If you kiss me and don't feel anything, I'll know for sure we're over."

{"Olivia, hurry up! You've got to get Malcolm out of here before Manny comes! There could be bloodshed if they're both here at the same time."}

"Fine, I'll kiss you this last time, but that's it! I'm sure this won't lead to anything. I just want you to know it's over—for good."

Malcolm pulled me close to him and squeezed me tightly. Sloppily he locked his lips over mine while thrusting his tongue into my mouth and then thrashing it wildly. I suppose he thought that was his way of kissing me passionately. However, his last-ditch effort to arouse feelings of desire in me was ineffective.

Gasping for air, I said, "There, are you satisfied? I honestly didn't feel what you wanted me to. So please, let's just end this now."

"Fine, but I hope Manny knows that what goes around comes around, and if you'll leave me for him, then one day there'll be someone you'll leave him for. Don't feel sorry for me, feel sorry for whoever falls in love with you!"

Malcolm walked out the door and I never heard from him again.

That departing statement only had moments to linger in my ears, because before I knew it, Manny was pulling up in the driveway. They had missed each other by mere minutes.

Following my description of the events that transpired between Malcolm and me, Manny and I spent a beautiful day together. He wasn't mad about the kiss, but he was a little unsettled by the fact that he didn't have a chance to confront Malcolm.

"What a jerk! How could he ask you for a kiss? I bet he was hoping that I'd come up and see the two of you. I wish I had gotten here earlier so I could have shown him why it was a mistake to even touch you again!"

I snickered at his obvious jealousy and told him that he had nothing to worry about.

"Malcolm did say something that bothered me though. He said that if I'd leave him for you, then one day I'd probably leave you for someone else. Do you think I could do that?"

Manny stated softly, "No, I know you could never leave me. Your heart is complete toward me, and you know there's no need to go anywhere else."

From that point on, Manny and I spent every day together. After work I'd go to his house where we'd watch movies, eat mint chocolate chip ice cream and make love. Rarely would we leave the vicinity of his duplex. A few days were spent at the beach and others out to dinner. However, early on, it was apparent that we liked being tucked into our own little cubbyhole where we could be alone and away from the world.

Days turned into weeks and weeks brought the day of my departure painfully closer. Our time together began to run out. For the first two months, Manny and I tried to avoid the subject of my moving to Lansing to enroll in Michigan State University. To combat that thought, we relished in each other even more than I thought possible. Soon I would be moving 80 miles away. Although the drive was only an hour and a half from Detroit, being apart for a second was agony for both of us.

Unbeknownst to me, Manny was planning a surprise.

One day, a few weeks before my scheduled exodus, Manny insisted he and I return from our date early. Although I didn't want our evening to draw to a close, Manny was adamant about taking me back home. Upon our arrival, I was astonished to find at least twelve *dozen* balloons floating in the backyard. They were tied to chairs and other objects, deterring an escape into the endless sky. Walking among so many balloons made me feel as though I were entering a cloud castle. The entire experience was whimsical and magical.

I turned to Manny and jumped into his arms.

"I can't believe you did this for me!" I screamed. "That's why you wanted to come back early! You were with me this whole time and you never let on! They're beautiful! Thank you!"

"I'd do anything to see that look on your face."

"What look is that?"

"The look that's a mixture of excitement, joy and innocence. You're even more beautiful at this moment."

Planting kisses all of over his face, I bubbled, "Manny, I love you. I love you. I love you…."

"This is only the beginning," Manny whispered. "I promise."

The next day, I discovered that Manny had more than balloons in his bag of tricks. As usual, we ended up at Manny's place, talking and seemingly hiding from the world. I had the feeling that something was on his mind, but my inquisition was futile. I began to get worried.

"What's wrong, Manny? You don't seem like yourself."

"I've been thinking about your move to Lansing." His voice was sullen. "The more time we spend together, the more time I *want* to spend with you. I never want you to leave."

"I know, but I thought we decided you'd come up to visit me every other weekend, and I'll come home on the alternate ones."

"The thought of you leaving is keeping me up at night. I need to know that nothing will ever come between us again. I want you to stay here with me. Move in here, Olivia—don't go."

His plea was heartfelt and sad. I hated saying what we both knew was true.

"Manny, I wish I could stay with you, but think about it. If I stay here and move in with you, I'm going to give up on an opportunity that I've been looking forward to for years. You know that I have a full tuition scholarship that I don't want to pass up. But I think that if I don't go and at least experience college life, I could end up resenting you in the long run. I never want either of us to give up on our dreams just to be together and then turn out hating each other after it's all said and done."

Briefly, Manny was silent—distant even. And then he replied, "I know you're right. I just feel like I've missed out on loving you for so long, I really don't know what I'm going to do without you."

"We're still going to be together. I'm forever yours, you know that."

"Well, I've got something that will help you remember that while you're gone."

"Really, what is it?"

Smiling, he went into a dresser drawer and pulled out a small black box.

{"I can't believe it, he's going to propose!"}

"Manny…what is that?"

"Open it and see."

Slowly, I opened the box to reveal a beautiful band of gold with an amethyst as the center stone, surrounded by small diamonds.

He remembered that amethyst is my birthstone! I thought. And then I exclaimed, "It's beautiful! I love it!"

"Are you sure?"

"Yes, I think it's gorgeous, but…."

"But, what?"

"What does it mean? Why would you spend so much on a ring…just for me?"

"First of all, you're worth it! Second of all, it means that I love you and I want the world to know it!"

"So, I guess you're not proposing?" I asked sheepishly.

"Not yet, Olivia. But trust me, *when* I do, that center stone will be a diamond and not an amethyst!"

From then on, Manny and I prepared for the upcoming separation with more confidence. We were determined not to allow anything else to come between us, not even the distance between Detroit and Lansing. Three days before I was set to leave, Manny pulled another rabbit out of his hat.

During one of our hidden moments at Manny's apartment, he revealed something wonderfully shocking.

"I'm coming with you."

"What?"

"I've given this a lot of thought and I've decided to move to Lansing with you."

"How? Why?" I could barely speak.

"I can't spend night after night longing for you. I need to be with you every day of the week."

"Manny, I wish that we could be together too, but you have a job and your own place in Detroit. How can you move to Lansing now?"

"I found out that my job has a sister company just outside of Lansing. I can apply for a transfer and move nearby."

"How long have you been thinking about this?"

"Long enough to know that I can't go through living 80 miles away from you. When I asked you to move in with me, I had a feeling that you wouldn't be able to do it; leaving with you was my back-up plan."

"I'm so incredibly flattered! I can't believe that you'd actually give up your life here—just to be with me! But I can't let you do that. Remember what I said before: I don't want us to give up on our dreams to be together and then end up hating each other when it's all said and done."

"I could never hate you, Olivia. And trust me, I'm not giving up anything! Finding you gave me more than I could have dreamed possible! And moving to Lansing with you would just make my new life solid. Besides, you can't stop me!"

"Oh, really! What if I don't want you to come with me?"

"Fine, if you really don't want me to come, then look me in the eyes and say so."

Bringing me close, Manny insisted, "Go ahead, tell me that it wouldn't make you happy if I came with you."

After a brief silence, I replied, "Honestly, Manny, I'd follow you to the ends of the earth and it makes me so happy that you would pick up your life and move to Lansing to be near me. I would love it if you came!"

"I knew it! It's settled then!"

"But promise me something."

"Anything."

"Promise that I'll never have to live without you again. Promise me that you won't regret this decision and resent me later."

"I couldn't imagine regretting the decision to move closer to you. Olivia, you are all that matters to me and you always will be."

"But what about your responsibilities here? What about your roommate and friend, Nate? You can't just desert him."

"Nate and I haven't talked in weeks! I don't know what his problem is! Don't worry; I'll work things out with him. I won't leave him high and dry. I'm sure it'll take a few months to wrap things up here. That'll give him plenty of time to find a new place to stay. *I'm going to make this happen*."

True to his word, Manny's determination was relentless. He began making plans to transfer his employment to a nearby plant in Lansing. He gave his landlord notice about his forthcoming departure, as well as revealing his plans to Nate. Everything *appeared* to be going smoothly, but all of a sudden the bottom began to fall out.

The day I was due to leave, Manny's car broke down. It was irretrievably damaged, leaving him with no transportation. Not only was he limited in getting to and from work, but it became virtually impossible to make the trip up to Lansing as often as he wanted.

Despite this set back, I still had to leave as scheduled. So after picking him up, my mom and I drove up to Michigan State University in East Lansing. I brought all of my earthly belongings with me to move into the dorm. I had very mixed emotions. When everything was finally unloaded and the good-byes were said, the reality hit me like a lightening bolt.

Tears began to swell in my eyes as I looked into Manny's.

"I don't want you to leave. I'm so afraid to be here by myself!"

"You'll do fine! You were brilliant enough to make it here and even land a tuition scholarship! I know you'll be great!"

"Maybe so, but how am I going to stay here without you?"

"Just remember, I'm on my way. I'll be here soon, I promise."

His words were comforting, but only for a moment. As my mother and Manny drove away, I felt as if I were beginning a sentence in prison! I sat on the bed and began to cry.

{"Pull yourself together! Today is only the beginning of a wonderful experience. Don't be afraid to live it!"}

I gathered my composure and began to unpack. Shortly thereafter I was interrupted by the arrival of my roommate. Our meeting was awkward. We were both embarking on a life that we weren't sure we wanted. Once the initial unpleasantness passed, we really hit it off. I went on about how much I missed Manny and she went on about how much she missed her parents. I realized that I didn't think of or miss anyone as much as Manny. However, talking to a neutral party helped. Slowly, I began to feel more at ease and decided to make the best of the situation.

Secretly, I resolved, *I can do this. I'll be patient and wait for Manny's arrival. He'll move nearby and then my life can really begin! Until then, I'll concentrate on studying and looking for a job! I can do this...I hope.*

Early on, I realized that college wasn't nearly as difficult as living so far away from Manny. Since he didn't have a permanent means of transportation, Manny had to either catch a bus to visit or bum a ride from a friend. Both methods were inconvenient. Sometimes friends couldn't be relied upon and other times, bus fare was scarce. We were both trying to save money for Manny to rent an apartment close to campus. The separation was extremely painful for us both, but Manny was grief-stricken by it. I began to see changes in him almost immediately.

Despite the fact that we spoke on the phone every night, Manny became even more possessive than before. If I was even a few minutes late calling him, or not in my dorm room when he would call, then Manny would conjure up several scenarios regarding my whereabouts. Usually—in his head—I was off with some other guy, at a party or just happily enjoying life without him. However, much of his anxiety came from wondering if I was safe or not. Campuses can be a very dangerous place for females, especially at night. So often Manny would be worried sick about me.

Although I was aware of his angst, I didn't realize just how deep it went, until one weekend when the truth surfaced.

After saving for months, Manny was finally able to save up the money to buy a used car. At that point, we hadn't seen each other for two weeks, so hurriedly Manny made plans for a visit. We spent a wonderful weekend together, talking, laughing, going for walks on campus and eating pizza! Every time we were together, the campus became a magical wonderland. However, when we were apart, college was more like solitary confinement.

On Sunday night when it was time for Manny to drive home, he insisted on staying.

"You have to go to work tomorrow, don't you?"

"Yeah, but I'll drive back in the morning before work."

"Will you be able to make it to work by 6:30am if you leave tomorrow morning?"

"Sure, I'll get up at 4:00am to make the hour and half trip back; that's plenty of time."

Assured by Manny's words, I agreed to let him stay another night in the dorm with me. I was more than happy to oblige, because whenever he'd leave, I'd cry for days afterward. However, that one night turned into two nights. Finally, Manny broke down.

Quietly tears surfaced in Manny's eyes as he told me, "Olivia, please don't make me leave! I can't live another day without you! I can't sleep, I don't eat and I can't think of anything except you!"

I was shocked by his admission, but I was also very touched.

"I didn't realize how hard it's been on you since I moved here."

"All I can think of is how happy we were this summer. Why did you have to move here? Why did you have to ruin what we had?!" Anger was revealed in Manny's voice.

"You know why I had to move here, we went over this! Why are you trying to make me feel guilty?"

"I'm sorry, I just feel so alone when you're not around."

"I feel that way too."

"Nate and I still haven't been getting along and the foreman at my job has turned my life into a nightmare! It seems like my whole world crumbled when you left."

"What about the money we were saving so you could move here?"

"I've saved a lot. Even though I spent $700.00 on the car downstairs, I still have enough for a security deposit."

"Well, I think I can swing first month's rent. I wish we could have stuck to the original plan so we'd have more to work with, but I miss you just as much as you miss me. Let's do it!"

"Good, I'll make a few phone calls from here and let my landlord know that the move is officially planned in two weeks. Nate already had notice; he's going to move in with his grandmother. I'll start looking for work today."

"I thought you were going to transfer to a plant nearby."

"I asked about that, but there were no openings. Don't worry, I'll find something soon."

From that moment, our lives spiraled out of control. We did find an apartment near campus, but Manny couldn't find a decent job. Lansing was more or less a suburb, quite a contrast from Detroit, where Manny previously had no trouble finding employment. A mixture of things was against him: his long hair that he always wore in a ponytail, his obvious minority status and the fact that he didn't have a high school diploma or G.E.D.

Although I had a part-time job, it was barely enough to buy books and food on the weekends when the cafeteria was off-limits. When I enrolled at MSU, I signed up for a meal schedule that included three meals a day, five days a week—no weekends. I assumed that I wouldn't be on campus many weekends and if I were, I'd have enough money to buy food for two days. Quickly I found out that was not the case. I had to take out a loan to cover my dorm fees and expenses. When credit cards were sent to me, I frantically took advantage of them just to maintain the necessities of life.

My mother rarely visited and I only received one care package from her the entire school year. She sent money twice, and called maybe once a week. I realized that once she dropped me off, she didn't look back. My father never visited—not once! The only time we spoke was when I would call him—he never dialed my phone number. The friends that I thought were for life never called, wrote or visited. And my visits to them only exposed that they had grown into different people. Other than Manny, I was completely abandoned.

Sadly, Manny would discover just how horrible abandonment felt. Despite the fact that he'd moved out of his parents' house and was living on his own, he and his mother still had a decent relationship. He and his father, on the other hand, were and would always be at war. When his mother found out that Manny planned to move to Lansing to be closer to me, she lay before him two brutal choices: "break up with Olivia and stay away from her, or move to Lansing to be with her and lose your family forever!" Basically, it was between me and Manny's family, his mother, brothers and sister. She admitted that she'd turn them all against him and that if he ever needed anything, she'd make sure no one would lift a finger to help him. It was the biggest betrayal Manny had ever experienced, but his choice was simple, from what he later told me.

"I'll never leave Olivia! Unlike you, she loves me unconditionally! If the tables were turned, she'd never make me choose between you and her. You never even gave her a chance! You judged her only by her skin color and that's it. It doesn't matter that she makes me happier than I've been all of my life! It doesn't matter that she's waited for me, trusted me and stood by me. None of that matters to you—only that she's black! Well, that's too bad. My decision is final! I'm going to stay with Olivia."

That was it; our families for one reason or another left us out in the cold—and what a brutal winter it turned out to be! The external stress of school, work and Manny's inability to find a job began to take its toll. When he first left Detroit and moved into an apartment a mile away from campus, Manny was beaming with joy and anticipation. We were embarking on a new chapter of life—together. We no longer had to live under the terms of our parents. At the outset, we were optimistic that our future together, though uncertain, would be everything we dreamed of.

A cloud of misery soon formed, eclipsing our optimism. After a few weeks of having doors slammed in his face, Manny began sitting in the apartment, drawing all day. If he wasn't drawing, he was exercising, but clearly he gave up looking for work. If unemployment wasn't bad enough, the used car he bought began giving us problems the first week after Manny's arrival. Daily, there were several automotive dilemmas; most importantly, the car would rarely start. Not only was he discouraged, but it also seemed as though the entire ordeal changed him. We began arguing relentlessly. At some point, I think we both wondered if being together was actually worth the battle we were fighting.

By the middle of the second semester, our circumstances had not improved. Manny was clearly defeated. And I lost hope in the power of love. I knew we loved each other. I knew that the love we shared was extraordinary. But I discovered the truth behind the adage, "sometimes love just isn't enough." Part of me wanted to keep trying, but another part—the sensible part had a conflicting point of view.

{"You're destroying each other by not facing reality. Manny can't stay here—there's nothing here for him. Soon, there won't even be you."}

As usual, it was as if Manny could read my thoughts, before I could even discuss my feelings, he verbalized my worst fear. "Olivia, I have to leave here."

One would think that I'd be relieved and that somehow we could work out a long-distance relationship, but something in his voice scared me.

"I tried to be the man you met. I tried to make things happen for us. I tried…."

"I don't blame you for anything! I know you gave everything you had. But now what?"

"You're right, I gave everything I had and I don't think there's anything left. The real me has been laid bare before you and I can't stand the thought of you seeing me the way I've come to see myself."

"What do you mean? I know we've been through a lot together, but what I see is that we need to regroup. If you go back to Detroit, find a job and a place to stay, we can start over."

"Is it that easy? I have nothing in Detroit—not even you! I can't go back there without you! I won't live like I did before, that means that all I did out here to be with you was for nothing, because we end up apart anyway!"

"I can't leave just yet, Manny, there's still time left in this semester…I…."

"I gave up my apartment, my job and my family to move here; why won't you sacrifice anything for me?"

"I begged you not to do those things! You insisted on making those decisions, no matter how hard I tried to talk you out of them! I'm not going to take the blame for what's happened! It's not my fault! I have a tuition scholarship; I even made a 3.5 grade point average last semester. I have to at least finish out this year and then…."

"And then I'll be gone. I'm leaving Lansing."

"What about this apartment? I still have a dorm room that's been pre-paid by the loan I took out, but I can't just leave all of these loose ends."

"Don't worry, I'll take care of everything. I'll let the building manager know we're moving out and I'll make sure all of the utilities are shut off. Since that's all you care about—loose ends."

"I care about you! I want you to go and make a better life for yourself, but I still want to be apart of it. I love you!"

"I love you too. So, *if…or when* you decide to come back, I can't say for sure that I'll be waiting. Living without you, Olivia, is painful, but living here is pure agony."

The lines were drawn in the sand. We loved each other, but we wanted each other on different terms—something had to give. Manny left to go back to Detroit at the end of the month and I went back to my dorm room.

Life as I knew it was forever distorted.

Chapter 21

The Journal—Part Six

Dear Journal,

My memories of Lansing were even more corrosive than I thought. As each event unfolded in my mind, I was propelled through a gamut of emotions. Consequently, my soul was stripped bare.

Every moment leading up to my relocation could be described as pure bliss. The truth about Manny's reasons for leaving was revealed. His feelings of deep love and longing for me were discovered. We looked forward to facing the future with love, trust and hope. Most importantly, he and I were ***finally*** together*! So what happened? Why was I allowed to taste the sweetness of this joy, only to have it dissolve right before my eyes? How is it that after everything we'd both been through to find each other, we ended up standing before one another, more lost than ever?*

Manny's return has flooded my mind with questions of "what went wrong?" Maybe, I just don't want to face the obvious answers. After winning the battle, we weren't equipped to win the war. We both fought the good fight, but as usual, I was left alone to suffer through the post-trauma. However, this time was different.

Before when Manny exited my life, I always knew in my heart that there was something keeping him from me. So when Manny revealed that he'd been breaking my heart against his will, our love was finally vindicated. I knew that if we were given half a chance we could live the experience of a passion unknown and out of reach to so many.

Once he was free of his family's influence, I was convinced there would be no force strong enough to come between us. The truth of the matter was, "we" were that very force. Manny and I were our own worst enemies. Maybe our intense desire for one another blinded us to the world outside of our dreams. We were trying to build a life together without knowing what 'life' was really about. I'll admit I was naïve. I think Manny was just stubborn. We simply could not navigate the harsh waves of reality. We were defeated by life—we never had a chance.

Manny's departure from Lansing left me cloaked in grief. Laboring through a fog of despair, I proceeded to complete my freshman year at MSU. Miraculously, I maintained a grade point average that earned my place on the honor roll. Despite my scholastic success, I decided to leave school at the end of the second semester. I just couldn't continue; I was no longer whole without Manny. The choice between an empty college experience and the fulfilling love of my life was no longer a difficult one. I chose love. Unfortunately, that decision came too late. When I got back to Detroit, Manny was gone. However, the man who would end up becoming my husband was there to replace him.

Since Manny's recent return to my life and my heart, I've asked him, "Why is it we could never get it right? Why is it there has always been so much tragedy and confusion shadowing our movements?" He was just as dumbfounded as I've been—no reply was given. Again, I begged him to release his hold on me. "It's too late. We had everything on Hoover and lost it all in Lansing; then you walked away again. Now that I'm married, you've resurfaced to claim what you think is rightfully yours. I'm sure my husband wouldn't see it that way." He told me that he'd let me go if I let him go—for good. So when my marriage became a source of pain instead of happiness, he knew I'd not only receive him, but I'd welcome him with open arms. "Until your husband gives you what I do, we'll NEVER really be over."

The clarity that Manny's words brought was somewhat comforting. On the other hand, I was tortured by the dilemma they presented. I was sure I couldn't have them both—Manny and my husband—it was either one or the other. So who would win out in the end? Manny, the most intense and passionate love I've ever known? Or my husband, the man I've shared my heart and life with for almost six years?

Manny or my husband? My husband...what about him?

Chapter 22

My Husband

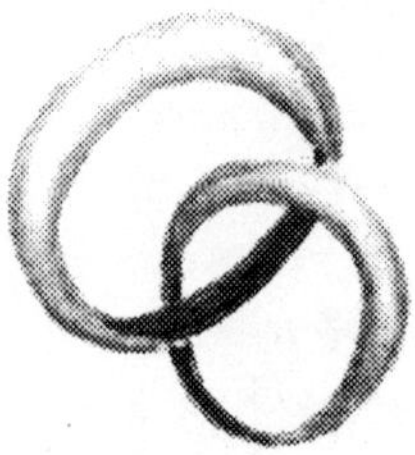

After giving up my college scholarship and returning to Detroit, I was brought to my knees when I found that Manny was no longer there. He'd left Lansing to pick up the pieces of his shattered life, but I guess that was easier said than done. The Manny I knew gave up on us and on himself. He was in no condition to receive me, so he didn't. In his mind, "Manny and Olivia" had been destroyed when Lansing hit like an atomic bomb.

Before Manny left, I knew I had a decision to make. I searched my soul for the answer and it didn't take long to figure out that my life, as tumultuous as it had been with Manny, was nothing without him. He'd given up his family, his job, and his independence to follow me to Lansing. In all actuality, he *gave up his very being to* ***be*** *with me*. However, my staying to finish out the semester spoke volumes to him. Apparently, he assumed that I'd chosen school over him—not choosing our love above all else, as he had done. That just wasn't the case. By the time I was able to prove that to him, Manny was out of reach. I could barely process the situation. I couldn't go back to college, my scholarship had been forfeited and I couldn't go back to live with my mother who was totally disappointed with my decision. Ultimately, I was propelled onto a new pathway, one that led to ***my husband***.

I met the man who would eventually become my husband around the same time I met Manny. With the whirlwind affair I was experiencing, it was no wonder that I barely noticed him. Upon my arrival back in Detroit, he became the stabilizer my world needed.

Our relationship lacked the fire and passion that Manny's and mine thrived on. This man had been through his own struggles and just wanted to settle down. He'd had trouble with family, friends and unemployment—much like Manny had experienced. The difference with this man was that he wanted to put the drama behind him and make a fresh start…with me.

Since making a fresh start was also my goal, we decided to move in together. We reasoned that if we just stuck together, we could get through anything. As difficult as it was to leave the past behind, slowly our pain lessened. Although life had been unduly cruel to us both, we realized it was possible for our disfigured souls to find love again. Eventually, he and I decided to marry. The entire experience was without fanfare. He didn't even propose. It was just an idea that had been floating around us like a cloud. We knew we could live together. We knew we were good for each other. And we knew we accepted one another, as we were—no games, no mystique—just us. We had found solace in each other.

"Let's do it, Olivia. We've been talking about getting married for months. What's stopping us?"

"We don't have money for a wedding, a reception or a honeymoon. No offense, but we're barely able to make the ends meet."

"If we wait to have money for all of those things, we'll never get married," he said with a smile.

I knew he was right. Besides we had everything we needed to make a marriage work that was the important thing.

"Alright, let's do it!"

{"Are you sure about this?"}

That voice had been inaudible for so long. After I lost Manny, I couldn't hear or feel anything. I think my pain drowned out the speakers in my head. Now that I'd been working through and getting over what Manny and I shared, that voice was back to haunt me.

{"If you marry this man, won't you be settling? Marriage is supposed to be forever. You can't just walk away from a commitment like this when things get rough—this is for life!"}

That voice, although annoying, always had my best interest at heart. I understood the point it was making, but I was secure in my decision. At the time, I was certain that this man and I were as good together as any two people could possibly be. To my knowledge, Manny was gone and was never coming back. I had accepted that.

Confidently and happily, we were wed in a small chapel in August of 1995. Incidentally, the day itself was beautiful. Usually August is the hottest, stickiest month of the summer, but that day was extraordinarily balmy and pleasant. The sky was blue and cloudless. It seemed as though the heavens gleamed with approval of our nuptials.

On our wedding day, I was only nineteen and my groom was twenty-one. Everyone we knew thought we'd never last. They were sure we were too young to see our vows through; however, our age never factored into our decision to marry. We both felt as though the life we'd lived up to that point had strengthened us for any future challenges.

"If we survived so much on our own, how much more could we endure together?" I was committed to our commitment and so was he. My new husband and I were bonded—forever.

"...My husband..." I secretly whispered to myself. "I have a husband!" I giddily laughed at the thought. Still, being married seemed to come very naturally to me. I enjoyed sharing my time and my life with "my husband." It was like I had my best friend by my side every day and every night. We'd talk for hours about our past, the present and what we wanted for the future. We'd laugh at each other's jokes and share popcorn while watching our favorite television show—*The Simpsons*.

On so many occasions, he'd chase me through the apartment with a crazed look on his face. God help me if I was caught! He'd tickle me until I could barely breathe. Of course, retaliation was the name of the game. We'd have so much fun trying to strategically outmaneuver the other person. If he tickled me into submission, I'd end up doing something even wilder, like pouring water on him while he slept. I made sure to lie in wait and when he would least expect it—I would strike!

That's just how we were with each other. We were more friends than lovers. Although we were newlyweds, our friendship seemed to overshadow any desire to romanticize our relationship. I blame myself for that. Intimacy became the act of a traumatized victim reliving a sexual assault. The fact of the matter was: nothing compared to what Manny and I had before Lansing. There was no passion, no tenderness and no act of physical love that could parallel the ecstasy Manny and I shared. My husband was not up to such a challenge. But it was more than that. The previous couple of years seemed to impact me in ways that I only became aware of after I was married. Memories of all the failed attempts at love and intimacy, as well as the years of molestation I suffered through as a child began to surface in a horrible way. Consequently, sex became less and less pleasurable to me and my husband became more and more frustrated. He tried to be compassionate and understanding, then again, he was tired of suffering for my past experiences. My lack of interest in sex became the catalyst for the future erosion of our union. Despite the problems in the bedroom, our daily relationship was still so strong that it would take five years of other marital discontentment to raise a red flag.

Throughout those years, my husband and I were intensely busy working. We were trying desperately to claw our way out of the pit of debt I'd begun digging in college. Unfortunately, our years together brought great depth to that pit and those financial woes began to take its toll on us. As much as we both worked, there was never any extra money. We rarely left our one-bedroom apartment because without money, outside activities were few and far between. Cabin fever often yielded discussions about money that most likely snowballed into heated arguments.

"You know we need to send the credit card company at least $100.00 this month."

"Why can't you send the minimum payment? That's just fifteen bucks, right?"

"Sweetie, I thought you agreed to a plan for paying off these three credit cards. We'd focus our attention on the smallest one first, pay it off and then move on to the next one. We agreed that if we keep sending only the minimum payment, we're not only throwing good money after bad, but at that rate, it'll take forty years to pay them off!"

"Why should I bust my ass at that plant, hauling and stamping that heavy steel over and over again, day in and day out—until I feel like putting my head in one of those die molds and letting it stamp my brains out—just to pay off *your* credit cards?" Those were obvious fighting words. This one was going to be bloody.

"Oh, *now* they're *my* credit cards! You weren't saying that when we were charging groceries! And what about that $200.00 total gym that you just had to have! You ordered it from an infomercial and you've barely even touched the damned thing! What about those things?"

Venom slinging like that became more and more prevalent as our time together rolled on. At first these types of arguments would start out fiery and then gradually transform into quiet talks. When the heat of the moment passed, we'd literally kiss and make up. We would dismiss the incident as our venting of frustrations about life—not each other. Each dispute was a learning experience, with that in mind; we would never go to bed angry. We were determined not to allow the anxieties of that day to spill over into the next.

"I'm sorry, Olivia. I shouldn't have said those things. I love you." His sincerity was genuine and that made forgiveness inevitable.

"I'm sorry too." My eyes would be swollen with tears and my voice would crack from having yelled so much. "Let's not fight like this again. I really hate hurting each other this way."

We'd both agree to a kinder, gentler way of handling difficult issues, but a cycle began to emerge. Monthly arguments turned into weekly ones, and soon daily battles surfaced. Insults, accusations and blames were flying everywhere.

By the end of the five years, our relationship was clearly strained. Throughout those years, I wondered if I'd made the right decision about marrying this man. On occasion, I'd think of Manny and miss our time together. Eventually, the occasional thought spawned into deep meditation and longing. Manny's impact on my life was still being felt. Soon those feelings unlocked the door and allowed him the opportunity to step back into my heart and my life.

Chapter 23

The Journal—Part Seven

Dear Journal,

Manny's recent return to my life has been a mixed blessing. The fact is I've been betraying my husband with Manny, and as bad as that is, somehow my relationship with him has been therapeutic. He knows me so well. Together, we've been journeying through the past: mine, his and ours. For as long as I've known Manny, I've never been able to conceal anything about myself from him. So, although I've tried to hide the truth, he ultimately sensed there was more to know than what I was telling.

He asked me the other day, "Olivia, why are you keeping things from me?" Hearing that question posed to me sent a shiver down my spine. I didn't answer right away. So he continued, "I know you. And for months we've been talking, not just about how things went wrong for us, and how we shouldn't be together now that you're married. But we've also gone over the problems you've been having with your husband. Something just doesn't add up."

At that point, I could no longer make eye contact with him, so again he spoke, "You know you can trust me, Olivia. And I trust you, but I know your problems go deeper than a '65 Bonneville, money problems and some unfulfilled promises. You need me and I'm okay with that, but I want to know ***why*** *you need me."*

His words were so gentle and comforting that I began to

feel guilt at having kept the entire truth from him. I suppose I've been talking around it, hoping I'd never have to actually tell anyone about it. I've never shared this secret pain with anyone and I wasn't sure if I could. Sharing my thoughts, dreams and desires with Manny was one thing, but exposing my enormous grief was another. With Manny, I had no pain, so if I told him, sorrow could seep into our forbidden yet safe sanctuary we'd found in each other.

Manny was not going to stop until he got what he came for; and that day, he came for my secret. He kept insisting, "You told me that you and your husband were having money problems. You even said that you'd been arguing a lot and at times that led you to thoughts of me."

I admitted that arguing with my husband made me vulnerable to memories that Manny and I had shared.

"But there's more, isn't there? I can tell. During these past few months, you've allowed me back into your heart and into your bed, but I sense there's a place that you won't let me into. I think it's time you take me there and show me what you've been hiding."

Manny's tender plea strengthened me for the painful process of revealing what my problems with my husband have really been about. I told him that the Bonneville, money troubles and feelings of neglect were mere symptoms of a deeper, darker, sinister disease devouring me from the inside out.

I started slowly, telling Manny about a happier time—when my husband and I bought our first home together. Soon, I was relating how changes were coming...changes that I just wasn't ready for...changes that changed me....

Chapter 24

Changes

Our five-year anniversary marked the beginning of a new era for my husband and me. Miraculously, all of our penny pinching and backbreaking labor finally allowed us the opportunity to purchase our own home. To our delight, we were approved for a small homeowner's loan. This modest amount permitted us to buy a small two-bedroom house with new vinyl siding, a one-car garage and a big backyard. It was a dream come true! In fact, I thought I was dreaming when we received the news that we qualified. But what made us both ecstatic is that we didn't have to come down with a large down payment, something we definitely couldn't afford. We only needed to pay half of the closing costs to move in—a mere $850.00! The credit card payoff plan which improved our credit rating immensely, coupled with the fact that we had what the mortgage broker called "family status," put us in a good position. Although we didn't have children at the time, the fact that we were married made us a family.

A family, I thought, *I finally have a real family, and now this family finally has a home of its own.*

The entire experience was rather profound for me. I had moved around so much as a child, never—ever—planting roots anywhere. The troubles with my father always made stability and security a fantasy floating on a breeze. Whenever I would get close to being comfortable at a residence or in a school, violence would erupt, sending us out into a world of uncertainty and unfamiliarity. Yet, when I was sixteen, I did receive a taste of a peaceful home life.

That's when my mother and I were living at that house where Manny tracked me down, *the first time*, after having been missing in action for a year. That serenity lasted for one year until my mother remarried, sending us on the move again. And then with another meager year's passing, I was sent out into the jungle of adulthood, being propelled into campus life in Lansing. Only nine months would pass before I was on the move again—on my own—having lost Manny and all hopes of optimism. That's why this house was so important to me. During those five years, my husband and I moved a couple of times, but now we'd be settled, together, in a real home.

If I couldn't grow up in a safe home, the least I can do is create one for myself and my children.

This house centered on my dreams of no longer running scared from my past, but looking forward to a bright future. I thought that by the time we moved in, all the badness was behind us.

"I mean, for something so wonderful to happen, we must have been doing some things right. Right?" I didn't expect a response, seeing as that I was talking to myself out loud while standing in an empty room.

{"Yeah, *some* things."}

I thought I'd put that voice out of commission years ago. Why was it back—again?

"I'm finally happy! I have a good husband and now we're moving into our own home. Just think we're both under thirty and we've accomplished something that many have yet to even attempt."

{"Who are you trying to convince?"}

I hated when that voice was so condescending!

"Now that everything has fallen into place, I can finally stay home and look forward to having children, like we decided."

{"Who is this 'we'? You and your husband or you and Manny?"}

"Where is this coming from? I haven't seen or spoken to Manny in years, how would I end up having *his* children? That's ridiculous!"

Just as quickly as that voice crept in, it scampered away.

"That was weird."

I dismissed the incident and resolved to focus on the moments my husband and I would share in *our new **house***. Those moments would turn out to be the happiest that he and I had shared since we were first married. Although, the pressures of life had changed us both so much, our home seemed to put everything back on track.

Soon after we moved in, I resigned from my position as a secretary. My husband's new job was sufficient to maintain our expenses. Of course, a two-income household would have been ideal, but he and I had a plan: purchase a house, resign my job to focus on our home and then we could try to have a child. We had been talking about having a baby for years, but now we finally felt ready. We had the house and there was even a little extra money coming in, our plan was on a steady course—until my husband changed everything.

Within weeks of our move, I noticed my husband's behavior became rather unusual. He had become distant and edgy. I knew work wasn't easy, but his new job was much less stressful than his previous position at the metal stamping plant. He was making more money painting cars at a body shop. At first, he was happy about all of the changes our life was undergoing, so I couldn't understand the sudden shift in his mood. I'd often try to talk to him about his attitude, but he'd deny there was a problem.

"Olivia, I'm just tired from work, it's nothing."

"You seem more than tired, you seem emotionally exhausted. I'm really starting to get worried about you."

"There's nothing to worry about! Stop nagging me!" he snarled.

I was shocked. I knew something was wrong. Arguing was nothing new to our relationship, but my husband rarely reacted negatively when asked about his feelings. We were really good about talking everything out…eventually. So I thought this time would be no different.

He'll come to me when he's ready.

{"You may not want to hear what he has to say."}

I got a sinking feeling when I heard that voice. I couldn't respond to it. Fortunately, it didn't press further.

Things were pretty normal after that day. In fact, I started to wonder if I'd been imagining any problems in the first place. My husband was more wonderful than ever. For two whole days, he was more loving, compassionate and attentive. I'd never been so content. Our marriage had its difficult times, but I felt that we'd really closed the book on our past problems and begun writing a whole new tale. And then one day, my husband came to me and…changed me.

He'd come home early from work one morning. I was in the middle of my exercise routine when I heard the door open.

"Honey, is that you?"

"Olivia." His voice shivered.

"Are you alright? What are you doing home? You've only been gone for two hours. What's wrong?" Questions spilled from my lips because I was afraid of the answers.

"I don't feel very good." He wouldn't look at me.

"What's wrong? Are you nauseous?"

"Yes." His voice shivered again.

"Sweetie, tell me. You're scaring me. Do you need something for your stomach?" I turned to leave. "I'll grab the Pepto."

"No. Don't leave. I have to tell you something," he said as he grabbed my arm.

"Okay, go ahead."

"Olivia, I've…I've thought about cheating on you before."

"What?" I said with a smile. "Is that what this is about? I'm not stupid, I know that men sometimes fantasize about other women, especially when they've been married as long as we have."

At first he didn't respond. Just as I put my arm around him, he began to weep.

"Oh my God! What is it?"

Through tears of obvious agony, he finally spoke. "Olivia, I'm so sorry. I have to tell you something."

My heart pounded as it sank into my shoes.

"I've never been happier. I don't know, I think it's this house and your being home. I never thought we'd make it this far. We've talked about having a baby and…and…now I can't do that until I tell you the truth."

I could barely speak. "What truth?"

He sobbed as the words poured out, "I…I didn't just think about cheating…I actually…I… I did it, I…I cheated on you."

Those words were a wrecking ball striking the room. I stood up. "What? What have you done?"

"There was a girl…and she and I...well, we didn't actually have sex…I think that's why I've been able to keep this secret for so long…because I kept telling myself that she didn't have me the way that you've had me…so I've kept it a secret…for so long."

"How long? How long has it been? How long did you do this with her? Who was this person?" The questions were endless. "How could you? I thought we were happy! Why would you do this to me? What did I do?" I fell to my knees in tears.

He fell down beside me and tried to put his arms around me.

"*Don't touch me! Damn you! Don't ever touch me!"*

His pain turned into fear. Quickly, my husband tried to explain, "Olivia, it was two years ago. There were so many problems then. You and I had been having trouble in the bedroom for so long, I was frustrated with my job and…I was an ass! I went out to see a friend of mine from work… remember that rainy day, when you worried because I'd been gone so long and I hadn't called. I told you that I was hanging out with my friend Tyrone and that he didn't have a phone…remember?"

"Yeah, so what! I remember!"

"Well, I went to see him and there was a little party going on, I went in and…well…um…there was a girl. I'd never met her before and…and we got to talking. She was flirting with me…and…well, you were so distant with me sexually. I…I…hadn't felt like that in so long…and—"

"*Oh, so it's my fault! That's what you're telling me! You BASTARD! It's my fault that you….*" I couldn't even say it.

"No, sweetheart!" he said, reaching for me. "You were always great, babe, always."

Pulling away, I said, *"Just not good enough on my back! Or maybe I'm terrible on my knees, which is it?"*

He looked shocked as he heard that description, I usually didn't talk that way. "No, it wasn't about sex, it was about feeling wanted, feeling like I was good, feeling like I was better than I really was."

"So, what happened?"

"I don't want to go into details."

"You'd better tell me whatever I want to know!" I was yelling through tears. *"I deserve to know!"*

"Okay, okay, I'll tell you. So we were at this party and she got...well, touchy-feely, she...she started rubbing my leg and...well... I told her I was married, but she said she didn't care. She wanted to go upstairs. She said she just wanted to talk and it was too loud where we were, so...so I followed her up to Ty's bedroom."

As he spoke, I felt as though I was going to vomit.

"...Then, we sat on the bed and she...asked if I wanted her. I don't know what I was thinking. Part of me, wanted to...so badly, but the other part remembered our wedding vows. I... I...was about to leave when she pushed me back onto the bed and sat on my lap. I told her that I wouldn't have sex with her. She didn't say anything, she...she just eased down and unzipped my pants...." He began to sob harder. "What the hell was my problem? I just couldn't stop her; I...I knew that it was wrong, but I just wasn't myself. She went down there...and oh, Olivia, I'm so sorry...."

"How could you let her? Damn it, how could you come home and not say anything? Why are you even telling me this now? Didn't you say this happened two years ago?"

"After she was finished, I...."

"You mean after <u>you</u> were finished, you son of a bitch!"

"I deserved that...you're right, after I was finished...reality struck! I pushed her off of me and I ran to the bathroom...I puked my guts out and cried on the floor. I knew that what I'd done was horrible, but I knew you'd never forgive me! You would always say things about cheaters, 'once a cheater, always a cheater.' You'd say that you could never forgive someone who'd betrayed you. And even though I had a sudden, but late revelation about how much you meant to me, I knew you'd never understand. God, Olivia, I just didn't want to lose you. I figured...it wasn't so bad because I didn't actually have sex with her. I got myself together and got out of there. I…I promised myself that I'd never take you for granted again and that you didn't have to know."

"So, you never planned to tell me! You planned to continue lying to my face every day of our lives!" I cried so hard, I couldn't see clearly. *"So why did you bother telling me now? You looking for a reason to get out of this marriage?"*

"No." His voice was low and labored. "It's just the opposite. I want this marriage more than anything! I decided that I would do everything in my power to make up for that night. I tried so hard not to take what we have for granted. I put it all behind me, but then…well, we got this house and then we started talking about having a baby…and I just couldn't do it…I didn't want a child like this…."

"So, you don't want to have a baby with me, but you're the one who cheated! That's rich!"

"No, no, you don't understand, I really want to have a baby with you. And that's when this feeling started to come over me. I've been lying to you and even to myself, but I couldn't lie to our child. I didn't want to start a new life knowing what I did. I knew I was taking a huge risk by telling you this. I knew that I was jeopardizing everything that I cherish because there probably won't even be a baby now, I'm sure you're not going to stay with me. But I had to tell you. This house was a new beginning and I couldn't let what I did infect it. You just don't know how much I've hated myself all of this time, but I had done such a good job of hiding those feelings. For the last two years, I hadn't been unfaithful. In my mind, I'd learned a valuable lesson that you didn't need to know about. But when we moved in here and you looked at me with such satisfaction and joy, it all rushed back over me. You started talking about our family and what that meant to you and I realized that it meant just as much to me to *be* a family and to *make* a family with you."

I sat on the floor listening to my husband of five years pour his heart out to me and I felt nothing. I was colder and deader than a corpse before an autopsy. I heard every word that he said, but I couldn't hear anything. Silent tears streamed down my cheeks and I felt more than betrayed, I felt truly unworthy of love. I became hysterical.

I began screaming, *"It's me! It's all my fault! I'm just not lovable! I'm just not enough for anyone to love with their whole heart and soul! I'm just not enough for anyone to love!"*

"Oh, Olivia, that's just not true! I'm the fool that just didn't realize what I had."

"No, I…I did this…I didn't want to have sex and you didn't feel wanted and…I pushed you away…and then there were the bills and the…the…everything that I could do wrong, I did. I've always done everything wrong. That's it! Because…because…now you…you have just been added to the long list of people who have let me down. I never thought that you would betray me! I thought that we…I thought that I…was good enough this time…for you…Oh God, I want to die!"

Those words cut through him. I could see it in his eyes.

"No, this is not because of you Olivia. If you decided that you never wanted to have sex ever again, I didn't have a right to betray our bond. I'm not owed an orgasm. We're partners in life and whatever you're going through, I'm going through. I've realized that now. But then, I was being selfish and thought that my needs mattered more than your pain. I am so sorry. Sweetie, I am so sorry."

He lifted my chin and looked into my eyes and I could actually see the remorse as if it was literally written on his face. Tears were flowing down his cheeks and then it hit me and so I spoke, "I never would have known if you didn't tell me." I was calm. "I can't believe that you've kept this from me for so long, but you could have taken this secret to your grave and for all of the reasons you told me, you didn't. If you had never spoken a word about this, I never would have suspected a thing—and you knew that. It's been two years and I haven't accused you of anything or questioned your whereabouts, so you knew that I was oblivious and that you were in the clear. And yet, you finally confessed. You'd gotten away with murder, but walked into the execution chamber and sat in the hot seat, waiting for me to throw the switch. You did that and you didn't have to…and that's why I believe that you *are* sincerely sorry for what you did."

Upon hearing those words, my husband grabbed me and nestled his face into my chest. "I love you so much, Olivia, and I promise I'll never, ever hurt you this way again. I would die first!"

Pulling away, I said, "Please don't think that everything is alright between us. I do believe that you are sorry, but I don't know if I can forgive you. I don't know anything right now, except I know you love me and you took a chance on that love right now."

"I'm not asking for your forgiveness this very moment, but please, don't leave me. Just let me love you. Just let me try to make you want to forgive me with each passing day. I'll keep my distance, I'll do whatever you need me to do, but please, Olivia, don't ever leave me. Just let me love you, please, Olivia, please just let me love you…forever."

I didn't speak. I fell into my husband's arms and listened to his heart as it raced in his chest. I knew that everything he'd said had been true; I just didn't know what to do next. I still loved him so much, but everything had changed. These changes were unbearable. I didn't know where to turn. I didn't know what to think or do or say. I was uneasy in my own skin.

Everything had changed for me and I just needed a way to put my heart back together. I allowed my husband the opportunity he had begged for. He wanted to *show* me he was sorry, not just tell me. I wanted that too. Slowly, ever so slowly, things began to get better, but no matter how normal life appeared on the outside, on the inside I was no longer the same Olivia. After it was all said and done, I had changed and I couldn't recognize my own reflection. I was going through the motions, but I didn't feel a thing. And then I remembered the only person who'd ever made me feel loved and safe and I wanted that feeling so badly that I let myself miss Manny all over again. I allowed myself to love him again. I thought that it was harmless, because he wasn't there, but then…he appeared and I was more vulnerable to him than ever.

Chapter 25

The Journal—Part Eight

Dear Journal,

The torture of revealing that secret was obvious to Manny. Because of our connection, he has a heightened awareness of my emotions and thoughts. However, that extrasensory perception wasn't necessarily needed. I spoke the truth through a veil of tears. Afterward, I sobbed in his arms.

Holding me close, rocking me gently, he whispered, "Olivia, I'm so sorry."

Even throughout our worse moments together, Manny never betrayed my love for him. He never put physical desire before my feelings. Manny may have hurt me in many ways, but my husband's infidelity topped them all. Some could say that what my husband did wasn't that bad—he didn't actually have intercourse with that girl. However, the problem goes deeper than that. He allowed someone to defile something so sacred: our vow, our commitment, and our marriage. Even still, the problem ran deeper. My husband made me a fool.

Through even more tears, I asked Manny, "How could I be so blind? How could I not see what he had done? I didn't notice any warning signs; I didn't see the difference in him. Why didn't I see?"

"You didn't see any warning signs because you didn't know to look for any. You didn't see because you didn't think there was anything there to see—except your husband and what you two shared."

Manny could always put things into perspective for me. He could always heal me. Although seemingly exhausted from lifting that weight from heart, I longed for Manny's touch. Knowing me as he always did, he sensed my yearning. Slowly and sweetly he kissed away my tears. Passionately and lovingly he eased my pain. Rolling smoothly through the sheets, we were intertwined gracefully yet lustfully. Making love with Manny always left me feeling loved. As heated and erotic as our exchanges were, afterward I only felt soothed and nurtured. As was his style, he nestled me tightly in his arms. For a while, I forgot why I had been crying in the first place. Being with Manny was like being in a far away land, unpopulated and unvisited. When he and I were together, we were truly the only two people in the world.

The quiet was soon broken. "Olivia, I don't want to hurt you." I looked into his eyes. "But I still don't understand something. If your husband was sorry—sorry enough to confess and beg your forgiveness—what happened? If there were plans to put your marriage back together, why is he busy in the driveway, neglecting you and acting like nothing happened?"

I wasn't sure how to respond. I didn't really know the answers. I wasn't sure where my husband got lost on the road to earning my trust. And I don't know where I got lost on the road to forgiving him.

"I don't know what happened exactly. All I know is that we fell into a routine of normalcy as quickly as we could. Soon after, that Bonneville became his first priority. Avoiding his promise became his first instinct. I guess I've just been too numb to care...until now."

Manny's return awakened in me so many sensitive nerve endings. Finally, I started to realize that I had to face the fallout. I had to deal with...the aftermath.

Chapter 26

The Aftermath

During the weeks that followed the confession, life took several unexpected turns. At first, the tension in the air was suffocating. I could barely stand to look at my husband, not to mention talk to him. Despite the obvious silent treatment being administered, he persevered. Lovingly, he attempted to redeem himself and ease my pain. However, everything appeared to me as a clumsy, feeble attempt to mask what had happened. I was not going to be won over easily. Each day was different. Some days, I was more talkative than others. But most days, I was too busy talking to that voice inside my head.

The news of my husband's infidelity traveled quickly to my subconscious. That voice arrived on the next train, looking to help me through my grieving process.

{"How could this happen?"}

Daily I was in tears, so hearing that voice was no surprise to me. I answered, "I don't know. I thought I did all the right things. I thought I made him happy. I thought *we* were happy."

{"No,"} the voice rebuked. {"How could you let yourself start thinking of Manny again?"}

I was shocked and angry by that accusation. Screaming at the walls, I yelled, *"I'm allowed! Damn it! I'm allowed! I can do whatever I want! Why shouldn't I? He did!"*

That voice slinked away and didn't pursue the argument, although I knew that wouldn't be the last time we'd speak.

One day, as I sat peering blindly out the window, I heard it again. {"Why won't you let him go?"}

"I need him now more than ever. I wish I'd ended up with Manny instead. I wish he were here."

The truth was, whenever I tried to wrap my mind around what was going on between my husband and me, I was propelled into a memory of love and happiness shared with Manny. Maybe it was a defense mechanism; maybe I just couldn't handle reality. I couldn't face what my life had become without him.

Eventually, my husband began to detect the futility in his attempt to gain forgiveness. As the weeks passed, our marriage settled into a calm, familiar routine.

"If I can just move on and forget, then I'll make it. I'll get through this if I act like nothing happened, just pick up where we left off."

It was obvious that things would never be the same between us, but I didn't care anymore. I just wanted the pain to go away.

"Since it won't leave me, I'll leave it—behind."

{"Don't be silly. Pretending, denying, running away—that won't solve anything."}

"I don't need your permission. I've decided. I'm just not going to think about this anymore."

Within days of that decision, I reached out to my husband, being intimate for the first time in several weeks. He seemed awkwardly content with my gesture. Surely he realized that I was different, but who was he to complain? It had already been difficult for me to perform in the past; the current situation made it almost impossible, but I was determined to put everything behind me.

Perhaps it was his guilt or the fact that my behavior was unnerving, but my husband began to withdraw his pleas for reconciliation. That unspent energy was soon turned toward outside interests...the result being a car restoration project of ridiculous proportions. The job was far beyond my husband's budget and degree of knowledge. Still, this obsession grew stronger, and with it, the canyon between us grew wider. A 1965 Pontiac Bonneville became my husband's new mistress.

Periodically, I would question him about his plans to rekindle our lost love. To make headway during those first stressful weeks, he promised me the sun, moon and stars. Incidentally, it wasn't the solar system that interested me, it was the plan to renew our wedding vows and make a fresh start.

He had once told me, "Olivia, I know I can't change what I did, but from now on, I want to change what I am to you. I want to prove to you that I'm committed to what we have. I want to start over. I want to renew our wedding vows, I want to marry you again."

At the time, I was so sorry I'd married him the first time, I couldn't think of doing it again.

{"So, why ask him about it, if it's not what you want?"}

Because I wanted ***him to still want it. I wanted him to still be sorry.*** I wanted him to *want* to make things right always—not just when the truth first came out.

"I thought we were going to get married again this year."

"Um…you remembered that?"

"It seems like I'm the only one who remembered."

"That's not it. I just thought you weren't too happy about the idea…and now…I've been…well…you know, putting a lot of time and money into the Bonneville…I thought…maybe next year."

"Oh, so now that you've got a ***new mistress***, you no longer plan to keep your promise to me."

"That's not fair, Olivia! Why do you do that? Why do you have to take us back to that?"

"Since a few months have passed, now I'm supposed to forget what you did? I'm supposed to pretend that I mean the world to you? How am I supposed to forgive you when you don't know how to stick to your promises?"

"That's not what this is about and you know it. You didn't care about getting married again. You're just pissed off because of the Bonneville. You hate that car!"

"No, I don't hate that car—I hate you for bringing it here! I hate you for hurting me! I hate you for not making things better!" I began to cry. "Just forget I brought this up! Just forget the whole thing!"

Sweetly, he rebutted, "I don't want to forget renewing our vows. I don't want to forget what we have. I just thought that maybe we're not ready for that. Maybe…you're not ready."

Turning to leave the room, I whispered, "You're right, I'm not ready and I'm not sure if I'll ever be."

{"You're trying to punish him."}

"Damn right."

As time passed, things began to worsen. If we weren't arguing, we weren't speaking, fueling my ever-growing flame of resentment.

"Olivia, why won't you forgive me? It's been six months, already! What do you want from me?"

"Six months, huh? That's all it takes! Six months go by and now everything is over and done with! You no longer have to be sorry and I no longer have to be hurt! I didn't know that six months was the official timetable! Thank you for clearing that up for me!"

"Why are you still here? Why did you stay if you don't want to make things right between us?"

"So, now it's my fault things aren't right! I didn't let some stranger go down there on me and—"

Abruptly, he cut in, "That's not fair, Olivia! Don't you know how sorry I am, don't you know that I love you with all of my heart?"

The room began to spin. {"What are you doing to this man? Why won't you let him love you?"}

I couldn't see straight. "I can't talk to you about this anymore. I can't talk to you right now about this…I have to go…."

And that's what I did. I peeled out of the driveway, not sure where I was going, but definitely sure I had to get away from that house. I ended up downtown at a small jazz club. There was a quiet crowd in a dark room with soft music playing. That was exactly what I needed. I ordered a drink and sat there for what seemed like hours. As I got up to leave, I spotted a familiar face from the corner of my eye. I turned to see…Manny sitting alone at a small table by the stage. The sight of him almost took my breath away. In the next few seconds, I was assaulted with so many thoughts.

Should I go up to him…Is he alone…Is he married…Will he remember me…Where has he been for six years…Does he still love me?

{"You can't do this. You have a husband at home waiting for and worrying about you."}

I scrambled out the door, although that voice's entreaty was not the reason.

"It's been too long. Manny has moved on and even if I still love him—that doesn't mean he still loves me."

Unbeknownst to me, Manny had spotted me as I walked out the door. So on my way to the car, I heard, "Olivia? Is that you?"

I was shocked to hear his voice again. I stopped in my tracks, unsure what to say. I turned and locked eyes with him.

Shyly, I answered his question with a question, "Manny, is that you?" Knowing very well that it was.

Walking up to me, he said, "It's me alright."

For a moment we were both silent. My heart pounded intensely. The bass drowned my eardrums. That must have been what kept me from hearing that voice interrupt.

"It's been so long, Manny, how have you been?" My voice quivered.

"It's been *too* long, Olivia, how have you been?"

Before I could answer, he grabbed my hand and gently kissed the finger that held my wedding band. I was so embarrassed. I felt like that schoolgirl falling in love with him all over again, but there I was married to some one else, and now he knew it.

"Beautiful ring," he said with a smile. "Do you want to go somewhere and talk?"

That ring, that *wedding ring*, didn't discourage him one bit! He acted as if he didn't even know what it represented, although I knew that he was well aware.

Still weak in the knees from the encounter, I could barely compose myself to answer. Finally, I said, "Sure, let's go."

"I'll drive."

Manny always drove. Everywhere we went together, he always had to drive. He told me once that if he couldn't control the machine he was riding in then he wouldn't ride in it! It made him almost ill to think of someone else behind the wheel. He had to be in control—

always! He definitely was, especially with me.

I wasn't sure where we were going, but before I knew it, we were at a small park that lay at the bottom of a huge hill. Taking me by the hand, Manny raced up that hill, laughing and pulling me behind him. I was laughing too. Enjoying the night, more than I'd enjoyed anything in years. When we reached the top, we plopped down together on a huge patch of grass and looked up at the stars.

"I've missed you, Olivia."

We hadn't seen each other or spoken to one another in years, but I could have sworn not a moment of time had passed.

"I've missed you, Manny."

I lay there on the top of that hill, wishing I could stay there forever. Although it was a cold March night, I couldn't feel anything but warmth, lying next Manny. We didn't speak for quite some time. Too much silence allowed that pesky little voice to rear its ugly head.

{"Six months ago, you were happy with your husband. Think about that—it's only been six months."}

I thought, *Six months ago, I was happy. Within days of celebrating our five-year anniversary, my husband and I had moved into our very first home together. We appeared to have overcome many obstacles, living quietly and contently in our new house for one measly month, before he shatters my whole world! Yeah, six months ago—I* ***was*** *happy with my husband!*

The quiet must have made Manny curious. "Olivia, what are you thinking about?"

Determined to ignore any further comments from that voice, I answered, "I'm thinking about—you. Why is it that whenever you come into my life, no matter how long it's been, you are still so in tune with me?"

"We're just like that together, *we're just like that.*"

As one would think, we didn't spend that much time chit chatting about time lost. Questions like, "Where've you been?" or "What have you been up to?" cut into our valuable time. I didn't ask him and he didn't ask me. It was, again, as if we already knew the answers. Besides, more important matters had to be addressed.

"I can see that you're married. That wedding band is a dead giveaway," he said, smiling. "But what I want to know is: when can I see you again?"

That was it. There was no further inquisition into my past. There was no explanation about his past. There were no "what ifs?" or regrets. Simply put: there was just now. That was what we both needed.

I took his phone number and told him I'd call as soon as I could.

"I'm sure I'll be hearing from you." He kissed me on the cheek and grabbed my hand. Walking back down that hill was like walking from the light into the darkness. The fact was, Manny was the dream and my husband was the nightmare.

We drove back to his car, and then I headed for home. I wasn't sure what was going to happen next. I remembered the argument my husband and I had before I left. He wanted to know why I was still with him if I was so unhappy. Now that I could see Manny again, what was keeping me tied to this marriage? Maybe I just didn't know how to say good-bye.

It doesn't matter right now. I'm just going to enjoy the bliss that Manny brings into my life and worry about the consequences later. That's what my husband did—enjoyed first and worried later. What's good for the goose is good for the gander!

When I got home, I was surprised to see my husband waiting up for me.

"I'm sorry, Olivia. I should be more patient. I'm the one who screwed up. Take your time. I want you to forgive me in your own time; I'll let you do that. Just promise me something."

"What?" I asked, somewhat annoyed.

"Promise me that there's still a chance for us. Promise that you haven't closed the door on me for good."

I wasn't sure what to say. My husband was unaware of my encounter with Manny and I was unsure of what my future would hold with either of them.

"I promise that I'll try to do better."

That was all I could say. My husband accepted those words. It was late and we were both tired, maybe he was just exhausted and didn't have any fight left in him. That was fine, neither did I.

I could barely sleep. As my husband lay beside me, all I could think of was Manny's touch. *I can't believe he's back! I can't believe we have another chance!*

{"Your husband loves you and wants another chance, what about him?"}

I don't know about him, all I know is that Manny is back and I'm not letting him get away again.

It was that simple. Manny was back and I was—again—willing to take him back. All it took was that one meeting and Manny and I were back together and back in love. Inevitably, the affair began with that one night.

Chapter 27

The Journal—Part Nine

Dear Journal,

This expedition through years of memories—most enchanting, but many heartbreaking—has culminated at this moment in time. I've arrived at the present on the train of the past. We've come full circle, Manny and I; we both knew it.

Up to this point, he and I were determined to live in our own holographic Garden of Eden. Inside that special place were only love and joy, tenderness and bliss. We never discussed commitments outside the realm we sought refuge in. Although, memories of each other were allowed, my husband and details about our life together were left at the gate. Manny never discussed his past life that didn't include me and I never asked. But after three months of recollections and lovemaking, he plucked fruit from the forbidden tree. He sought the truth about my sorrow and inquired about my secrets. That was a turning point for us.

After finally revealing the facts about my husband's infidelity and eventual breakdown of our marriage, Manny was incited to probe further. The more we talked the more I realized he was searching my heart for something and was on a mission to find it.

I had already exposed so much. Throughout several weeks of secret rendezvous and intimate emotional and physical exchanges, Manny never seemed to care about my husband at all. Now after hearing the truth about him, Manny became more curious than ever.

"Olivia, you just told me that the night you and I found each other again was the same night your husband asked you a very important question, one you have yet to answer. So, ***why did you stay with him****, if you couldn't forgive him?"*

Looking away from his eyes, I spoke, "I couldn't answer that question then and I can't answer it now."

"Okay, I can understand why that night you couldn't answer him, but what about now? You and I have been together for three months, if you can't forgive him, and you love me, then why stay?"

That question blasted through me like a bolt of lightening through an old sycamore tree. I was stunned by his blunt take on the matter.

"You make it sound so easy, Manny, but it's anything but. We've talked about what went wrong with us in the past, why do you think it's so simple for me to leap from my husband's betrayal to your uncertain, but open arms?"

"I suppose I deserved that." Manny was hurt but still unwavering in his attempt to change my perspective. "But I never cheated on you, Olivia, and I never would."

Tears came from an unknown place. As they quietly streamed down my face, I said to him, "Really, do I deserve the happiness you claim you'll give me? We've been having an affair for three months; my husband had a momentary lapse of judgment. The fact is I'm worse than he ever was."

Manny didn't want me to look at things that way; he grabbed me and held me close to him. "You've been devastated and what we share is nothing to be ashamed of."

I started to be comforted by Manny's reasoning. Despite my feelings of guilt, I was still resentful of my husband's impropriety and of his new mistress...Lady Bonneville.

Chapter 28

Lady Bonneville

As my love affair with Manny progressed, my husband's love affair with the Bonneville progressed just the same. Stolen moments with Manny paralleled my husband's trysts with what I came to call "Lady Bonneville." She was what my husband put his heart and soul into. I'm sure if he could have he would have put something else into her also. I hated watching him pour so much energy into something that could not love him back. I was shocked at my own jealousy.

One night I awoke to find an empty space beside me where my husband usually lay snoring peacefully. I was surprised by his absence and immediately began a search into his whereabouts. It didn't take long to find him. The light from the garage led me to his exact location.

"Olivia?"

"Yeah. Didn't think I'd find you out here this late."

"Well, I couldn't sleep."

"Oh, so you thought you'd sneak away for a little private time with the old girl."

"Something like that."

"Well, I just wanted to know where you were. Now that I've found you, I'll leave you two alone." I was annoyingly sarcastic.

"Olivia."

"Yeah."

"Why don't you sit with me for awhile?"

"Well, I don't know, I'm kind of tired. Besides, if I was the one you wanted to sit with, you would have stayed in our bed and woken me up—not come out here to be alone with…her."

"How can you be jealous of a car?" he asked with a slight grin.

"It's not just the car…it's more than that and you know it."

"I don't know what it is anymore. I know things have been strained between us and ever since I bought this car; it seems to have gotten worse."

"Well, if you know that, why don't you do something about it?"

"What do you want me to do?"

"I can't tell you that."

"So let me get this straight. You want me to do something, but you won't tell me what it is. Why is that?"

"If I tell you, then you'll only be doing it because I told you to, not because you really knew what I wanted and did what I wanted you to do."

"What?" My husband chuckled. "You know that you're not making any sense, don't you?"

We both laughed out loud. After a few seconds of giggles, we stopped and looked over at each other. It was the first time in a long time that we actually looked *into* each other's eyes. The intensity of the moment was just too much for me to bear. I could hear my heart pounding in my ears. He moved in to kiss me when I looked over at…*her*.

"We'd better not; she'll see us. And if she's anything like me, she won't want to share her man with anyone." Those words marked my exit.

I returned to bed alone.

That was just one of the many times that I could feel my husband penetrating my defenses, ultimately sounding the alarm to fortify my arms and strengthen my resolve. I just didn't trust him. Or maybe I just didn't trust myself.

I'm not going to be made a fool again. I'm not going to give myself to him completely, just to have my heart ripped apart again. I was flooded with emotions. Anger began to build.

Curled up on the bed cradling a pillow, quietly weeping, I said to myself, "Besides, I'm not the one he wants. I'm not all he thinks about—maybe I never was. There's someone new in his life now."

{"If you can have an ongoing affair with someone, why can't he?"}

I hated that voice intensely for that. It always put the truth right before my eyes.

{"You shut him out months ago. So what if he turned to this car as some kind of solace, you're cold as ice most of the time. Just be glad 'Lady Bonneville' isn't flesh and blood."}

I ignored that sword of fact sticking out of my back and slowly drifted back to sleep.

On another occasion, I stood peering through the back window in our bedroom, watching as my husband vainly attempted a major brake repair, or so I thought. I don't know much about cars, but I do know a lot about frustration. I watched as he banged his knuckles as he searched for tools that were out of his reach or tucked away in the garage. I watched him get aggravated when a rusty bolt seemed immovable, despite his brute strength. I watched my husband have his own affair right in our driveway.

{"Why are you watching him?"}

"Leave me alone."

{"Leave him alone. Set him free, Olivia. You got who you want, Manny, what do you need this man for?"}

"Stop taunting me," I said as I left my perch.

{"You want them both, don't you?"}

Before I could rebuke that accusation, the side door burst open. By then I was in the kitchen and saw my husband as he barreled passed me holding his forehead. I had no idea what was happening because I had stopped looking out the window, preoccupied with my inner debate. Curiosity was first on the scene, but then concern quickly arrived to take its place.

"What's going on?" I yelled out. There was no reply. "Is everything alright?" Still, I heard nothing from him, so I went searching through the house. I found him in the bathroom, sitting on the floor with his head down.

"Why did you run by me like that? Did you need to use the bathroom that badly?" I chuckled. But he was unresponsive.

"Okay, tell me what's wrong with you? Why didn't you answer when I called out to you?" Still, he wouldn't respond or lift his head.

I began to get and sound annoyed. "Forget it then."

As I turned to leave, I heard a whisper, "I fail at everything."

"What? Why would you say—?"

As I turned toward him, he lifted his head, exposing the problem. Blood was pouring from a gash on his forehead. It had dripped down his nose, his lips and his chin. He was covered in it.

"Oh my God!" My heart raced. "What happened?"

I didn't allow for an answer, I sprang into action. I grabbed the first aid kit and the cotton balls. I sat beside him and looked at the cut. As I began cleaning it with antiseptic, I looked into his eyes. Tears spilled down his cheeks. I was stunned by the sensations that hit me.

"Sweetie," I said gently, "what happened?"

Finally, he related the events. Apparently he was trying to fit some new rims on "Lady Bonneville" when he discovered that the five-hundred-dollar rims didn't fit on her. He erupted and threw one of the rims toward the garage. Incidentally, before the rim left his hand, he pulled back to propel it when it struck him in the head, slashing him right between the eyes.

"Does it hurt that much?"

"No. I'm just tired of failing."

"What do you mean by that?" I asked.

"I've failed at everything I've ever tried, including us…especially us."

By the time he made that statement, I was done bandaging the wound. I could see where the conversation was headed and I wasn't sure if I was ready to go there.

"Olivia, I can't believe what a screw up I am." He began to weep.

"It's just a car, honey. You'll fix the problem, or you'll get new rims. I'm sure it'll work out."

"I don't care about that."

"I know how much Lady Bonneville means to you. This is just a setback. I promise, everything will be alright."

As I began to get up, he grabbed me.

"Why are being so nice to me?"

"What? You're hurt, I'm helping you. That's what a wife is supposed to do."

"Oh, for a minute, I thought that maybe you still cared about me."

"Of course I care about you, you're my husband."

"Lately, I've felt like a stranger in my own home. I've felt like a stranger in my own life."

"Well, I'm sorry, but…."

His eyes were still filled with tears. "I just thought for a minute, you were really worried about me. I just thought for a split second you loved me…you know…like before."

"I…."

He got up and walked passed me out the bathroom door. Shortly thereafter I heard the front door slam. I looked out the living room window and saw him driving away.

"Damn it!"

{"What do you care?"}

"Stop it!" I screamed.

{"I guess you don't appreciate Lady Bonneville being such a bitch!"}

After hearing that voice say such a preposterous thing. I laughed out loud. "Yeah! She is a bitch, isn't she?"

{"You still love your husband, now you just have to let go of everything else."}

I didn't argue. I just sat on the floor thinking about all of that blood. I was really afraid for him and for that brief instant, I didn't think of his infidelity; I didn't think of being hurt or angry; and I didn't think of Manny.

"I was scared that he was really hurt."

{"You were afraid that maybe, just maybe, you were going to lose him after all."}

"I don't know what I'm feeling anymore. I'm just exhausted."

{"It takes an enormous amount of energy to love them both. Eventually, you're going to have to choose."}

This time that voice was calm and soothing. I needed that voice—no matter how brutally honest or sappily sweet. I needed it to help me gain and maintain perspective. I needed someone to help me sort everything out. I needed to make a life altering decision that would have to be ultimate and unwavering. Most importantly, I needed to tell them both the truth about my feelings...and each other.

Chapter 29

The Journal—Part Ten

Dear Journal,

This entry is difficult for me, because for the first time, I lied to Manny. Or rather, I lied by omission. I've always been upfront about my feelings of jealousy and neglect due to what I've dubbed "Lady Bonneville." Manny has known from the start that I've felt as if my husband cared more about restoring that car than rebuilding our shattered marriage. However, when relating events surrounding my husband's mechanical mistress, I inwardly relived intimate moments that arose between my husband and myself. Outwardly, though, I was secretly very selective about those memories.

I didn't want Manny to find out that I had been so close to giving in to desires of reconciliation. In fact, I didn't want Manny to become aware that there existed such desires at all. I was unsure why that was.

This time, my relationship with Manny seemed to mean more to him than ever. At this most inconvenient and inopportune time, Manny was determined not to lose me. As my relationship with my husband slowly became less awkward, my relationship with Manny began to take on an uncomfortable feel.

"Olivia," Manny gently approached me one day, "I want us to have a life together. I want us to be more than lovers. Leave your husband and marry me."

Those words ushered in a whole new world of complications....

Chapter 30

Complications

At the onset of my affair with Manny, there was seemingly an unspoken agreement to live each day and love each other in the moment. It was understood from the beginning that I was married, and despite problems with my husband, I had not made a decision to walk out on him. In fact, I never thought that far ahead. I was so distracted by my self-imposed righteous indignation that I didn't take the time to consider anyone else's feelings—not even Manny's. He's been so eager to soothe, console and ultimately win me back that the circumstances surrounding our relationship have become clouded. The invisible boundaries were crossed.

Having just been embroiled in one of the most intense lovemaking experiences of my life, Manny turned to me and revealed his true intentions.

"Olivia, I want us to have a life together. I want us to be more than lovers. Leave your husband and marry me."

As heartfelt and genuine as those words were, they were equally shocking and disturbing.

I couldn't speak.

{"Uh, oh!"}

That voice said it all. I couldn't respond to Manny's proposal right away, so I got up from the bed and reached for my clothes. The room was silent as I dressed. At last, I spoke, "Manny, I thought we were just…well…I thought we were just living for the…stolen moments. I never thought you'd want to take such a huge step…I mean, well…you've never stayed with me long enough to make future plans, I didn't think this time was any different."

"Can't you tell that I'm different?" His eyes danced with excitement. "When we first started seeing each other again, it was obvious how much you needed me, but now I've realized how much I need you too. I don't want to lose what we have. Olivia, I don't want to lose you."

With each expression of love and commitment, I found myself in a state of distress, thinking, "Why aren't these words coming from my husband? Why has Manny realized all of this now—and not then—when I was free—when I was his and his alone?" Despite those thoughts, I didn't offer a reply.

Manny jumped from the bed and grabbed his clothes, speaking quickly as he dressed, he said, "I know this seems like terrible timing. I know I should have realized all of this stuff before…before I left Lansing."

{"Man, he's good! The original mind reader stands before you."}

I ignored my inner sarcasm and focused on Manny's next statement.

"I'm leaving for now. But I'll be back. I want to give you time to think about what I've told you." Walking over and gently pulling me closer, he whispered, "It's not a difficult decision. I adore you, Olivia. I'm here for you and I'm not going anywhere. Our connection is deeper, sweeter and more fulfilling than anything you've ever experienced in your life. Trust that, trust me."

Those words marked his exit; he gave me one week to mull things over. This situation paralleled the past so distinctly that I began to feel ill.

It's Malcolm and Manny all over again.

{"Yeah. So many years ago you had to choose between a guy you liked and the man you loved. Now you have to choose between the man you love and the man you're married to."}

I'm reliving that time all over again, but with much worse consequences. Breaking up with a boyfriend to be with Manny was harsh, but leaving my husband—that's just cruel.

{"It's only cruel if you care what happens to your husband. It's only a problem if you don't want to leave him. It's only an issue if you want to make your marriage work."}

That voice was right again! If I didn't want my husband, the decision would be simple. Deciding between Manny and Malcolm came easy to me; during that dilemma, I truly believed I belonged with Manny. Now I was not so sure. It's true that there had been serious marital dysfunction recently, but there had also been five years of endearing, warm and tender moments. This decision was not going to be made effortlessly.

Before I knew it, I began to feel weak and faint. Nausea hit unexpectedly. I thought I was just feeling unnerved by the bomb Manny dropped before he left. Suddenly I found myself running to the bathroom, barely making it to the toilet when I violently began to vomit.

{"What the hell is that all about?"}

I wondered that myself, but I didn't have long to ponder when I heard the front door open.

"Sweetie? Where are you?"

Quickly scrambling to flush the evidence down and compose myself, I rushed to my feet.

"Olivia?"

"Yeah. I'm in the bathroom, I'll be out in a second."

My husband had just arrived home, missing Manny's departure by a mere ten minutes.

"Hi."

"You look like crap!"

"Thanks!" I said while pushing past him.

"What's wrong? Are you sick?"

"Yeah. I've been feeling a little queasy. I think I'm coming down with something."

"I saw the bed was still a mess, have you been trying to rest all day?"

{"A…yeah…that's what you did."}

Shut up, I inwardly rebuked and then answered my husband. "Just for a few hours. I started feeling sick so I went to take a nap. It's no big deal. I probably ate something that didn't agree with me."

"Well, whatever it is, go lay back down. You don't look so good. Maybe I should call the doctor."

"No, no, I'll be all right. But maybe I'll just go back to bed. I'll see you later, okay."

I really thought I would see my husband later that evening, but I slept until the next morning. By the time I struggled out of my slumber, he was long gone, to make it to work by 7:00 a.m.

"What's going on with me?"

{"It's probably just stress. This stuff with Manny and your husband is probably going to kill you!"}

"Very funny."

{"Seriously though, you should really think long and hard about what this situation is doing to you. You're only one woman, with two men. You aren't wired for this type of excitement."}

As tirelessly relenting as that voice was, I could rarely find fault with it. I started to think that maybe I needed to simplify my life. Regardless of the issues my husband and I faced, I really didn't feel ready to turn my back on him and my marriage. However, Manny's love was valued in ways that were incomparable to any others. He could always be counted on to make me feel as though I had been set a side to be loved gently, delicately, and perfectly.

"Could what I share with Manny really survive in the real world?"

Again, my meditation was interrupted.

"Olivia?"

"Sweetie? What are you doing home from work?"

Smiling as he stood before me, he answered my question with one swift motion, which revealed the flowers hiding behind his back.

"Roses!" I shouted. "That's so sweet!"

"I knew you weren't feeling well, so I left work to cheer you up. Are you feeling any better?"

What was I supposed to say? That I felt as if I had lead for blood or that I still wanted to hurl pretty much every time I opened my mouth?

"I'm fine. No need to worry. I'm fine."

"Well, why don't I make some breakfast? You haven't eaten yet have you?"

The thought of breakfast brought bile to the back of my throat.

"Um, I ate already. Why don't you head back to work? I'll be fine."

"No. I planned to take the rest of the day off so I could nurse you back to health."

I didn't put up much of a fight to get him to leave. I was tired, but most importantly, I was really glad my husband was home. His sincerity was refreshing and reassuring. The fact that he *wanted* to take care of me made me feel like a true priority in his life. That day, I was no longer being neglected; I was being nurtured.

I slept a lot and ate very little. Later in the day, we watched some movies, but I started to feel sick to the stomach again. After puking my guts out a couple of times, I decided to just go back to bed. My husband stayed by my side the entire day. He was very patient and supportive. At one point, I was sure he'd been watching me as I slept because when I opened my eyes he was sitting in a chair across from the bed staring at me.

"How you doing, gorgeous?"

"Better. Maybe this bug is working its way out."

After eating a light meal, I was back to bed for the rest of the night.

The next day, I felt a tad bit stronger, but still not my best. My husband had to return to work, so I decided to run some errands despite my unsettled stomach. When I looked at the calendar to check some appointment dates, I came across some information that caused the room to spin.

{"What's that?"}

"Oh, my God!"

{"Olivia, this month…this month you didn't put in your code. You know, your secret code you use every month when you start your…."}

"Oh, my God!"

That voice was right. The little code letters I use to mark the beginning and end of my period were not on the calendar for this month and the month was pretty much over. I always wrote in that event, the first week of every month.

"It can't be. It can't be."

{"Oh, my God!"}

"It can't be."

{"You've been sick for the passed two and half days."}

Staring at the calendar, I whispered, "It's almost three weeks late."

{"Olivia, could it be?"}

I had to sit down.

{"You have to find out. Go and get a test. That way, no one has to hear about this if it's nothing. Go and get a test."}

"How can this be?"

Looking back, it was easy to forget, especially with all the stress I'd been under. Between maintaining my wifely duties and carrying on an affair with Manny, one could forget a little thing like a menstrual cycle—not to mention a birth control pill here and there.

"It's just stress. Stress can cause a woman to miss or be late with a period."

{"Can stress cause you to be fatigued and nauseous?"}

"Sure! Stress can kill you! What's a little fatigue and nausea?"

{"You're reaching."}

I *was* reaching.

I got up and drove to the nearest drug store. Along the way, I couldn't think of anything except "what if?" I rushed through the line and made it back home in record time. I was glad there were no cops on the prowl. On top of breaking the sound barrier, I was sure I broke a few traffic laws along the way.

Taking the pregnancy test out of the package, I repeatedly said to myself, "It's just stress. It's just stress…."

Trembling, I followed the directions and peed on the stick. I walked out of the bathroom, leaving the test behind to calculate the results.

"It's just stress."

{"What if it's not just stress? Olivia, what if you're going to be a mama?"}

If I tackled that question then I'd have to tackle another more difficult one. I wasn't ready to make the leap.

Slowly, I entered the bathroom; I peered over onto the sink where the test lay. "Two lines mean positive, one line means negative." I closed my eyes, took a deep breath and opened them…to find staring back at me…*two blue lines*. I stumbled and almost fell to the floor.

{"Olivia, you're going to be a mama."}

"Oh, my God!"

Those two little blue lines represented two complications: *Whom should I choose? And who is the father?*

{"Hopefully, they'll be the same person."}

Chapter 31

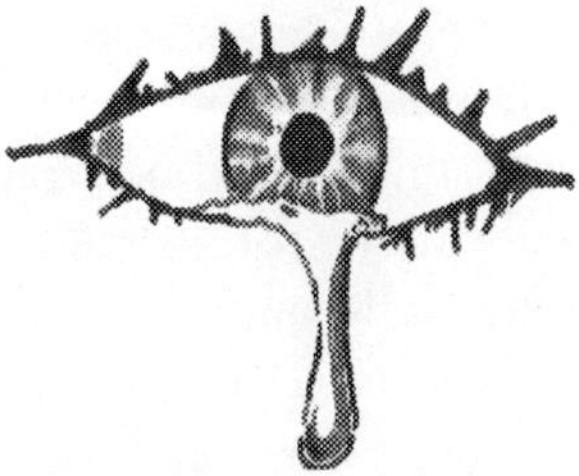

Reflections

While sitting on the bathroom floor rocking slowly back and forth, holding myself tightly, I had time to reflect on my current situation. The facts were clear. I had been married for close to six years, our anniversary being just a couple of months away. Despite the duration of my marriage, my husband and I had not been in sync for months. (Finding out about a spouse's infidelity can do that to a relationship.) I was also deeply engrossed in a love affair with someone I could easily deem the love of my life. To make a disastrous situation even worse, I was staring at a pregnancy test that displayed a positive result.

"I'm pregnant." I think I had to say it out loud to hear the words bounce off my ears.

{"Yeah. How about that?"}

That silly voice was being just that—silly. I suppose the entire ordeal was perplexing—even to my alter ego.

For at least an hour, I sat on that floor, rocking back and forth, thinking, reflecting, meditating, wondering what to do next.

Suddenly, the inner me took over.

{"Who do you think would make a better father, Olivia, honestly?"}

"Honestly?"

{"Yeah."}

"They're both wonderful men, but each of them have outstanding qualities that outshine the other's. Manny is passionate and romantic and tender and—"

{"Sounds like you're describing the better ***lover*** to me."}

I couldn't deny it. The qualities that stood out in my mind about Manny served a selfish desire that lived within me. "You're right. I am getting off track. Even though tenderness is a special quality that I think every father should possess, there are things about Manny that just don't suit the role as much as I would like."

I had to face it; Manny had never proved he had staying power. He would leave me at a moment's notice. Although he would have a seemingly good explanation, I often felt abandoned by him.

{"But you felt and still do feel loved by him, right?"}

"Yes, but I've just been so confused lately. With everything that's happened between my husband and me, I haven't been thinking straight. When I started this affair, I never thought things would end up like this. Manny wants me to leave my husband and marry him. To top it all off, I'm pregnant and I don't know which man to congratulate!"

{"You and Manny share a sensational history and a strong bond. You two could build a life together based on that."} The voice was actually pleading Manny's case, or was it?

"Yes, we have a ***history***. A past filled with memories of love and love lost, but," I dropped my head as I spoke to the walls, "he has yet to prove that he can be trusted."

{"Let's not start on trust. Your husband has proved that he can't be trusted."}

"But that was different. Even though he did that yucky thing with that girl, he came clean. And even though I've been treating him pretty badly, he's stayed with me every step of the way. In fact, if he hadn't been unfaithful, I may never have realized just how much he'd do to hold on to me."

{"So, you're justifying what he did?"}

"No, I'm just saying that he made a mistake and he's tried really hard to make up for it. I know I haven't made it easy on him, but he's been here putting in time and putting forth effort."

{"What about that car?"}

"Well, that was a blow to my already dejected self-esteem, but the question was, who do I think would make a better father? I don't believe this or any other car project would be a priority over my husband's child."

{"How can you be sure of that?"}

"It's obvious from the way he's been treating me these last couple of days. The more opportunities there are to take care of me, the more he makes himself available. Now, a baby needs plenty of attention and care, he'll rise to the occasion, just like he has with me."

{"So what you're saying is: the more you let your husband get close to you, the less time he spends with Lady Bonneville."}

"It seems that way. He's been a lot more attentive since I've been too sick to fight him about…." My mouth fell open; I couldn't complete my thought—out loud.

{"Olivia, I think you just got it."}

I think I did too.

{"The more you ***let*** your husband love you, the more loved by him you feel. You've been barricading yourself behind walls of anger and pacifying yourself with this affair with Manny. You're hiding and you're hoarding."}

"Hoarding? I don't get that."

{"You're hoarding your love, keeping it locked away for Manny, when your husband is the one who's been here aching for it, searching for it, begging for it. All Manny did was show up at the right place at the right time. He didn't have to earn your love again, you just handed it over. I hope you've finally figured out just how unfair you've been."}

Ironically, it was something rather simple that drew me away from this dialogue—I had to throw up again. In the midst of it, I didn't think of anything except how much I wanted it to stop, but afterward, a new perception crystallized.

I began to splash cold water on my face when I looked up into the mirror, facing myself, my own eyes, for the first time in months and that's when I began to think of…my baby. I was so consumed with the chaos my life had become that I didn't allow myself to consider the point of view of the most innocent and precious participant. What kind of father did this baby deserve? What kind of home should he or she be brought up in? Who would love it, unselfishly?

"I've finally figured it out."

{"Gee, I hope so. The writing's been on the wall for months!"}

"The past can no longer be the deciding factor on how I prepare for the future. I've gone back through time, hunting for answers and searching my soul. I've been frantically, reliving major events of my life, trying to find where in time I lost it."

{"Lost what? Your mind?"}

"No. Where I lost my essence, the true sense of myself. If I can find the strength to make peace with the past, then why not make peace with my husband's past as well? I said several months ago that we were a family. That's truer now than ever. There's a baby on the way, and this is its home, its family. I refuse to compromise my child's future because I won't stop letting the past hurt me."

{"He or she is going to need your protection and guidance."}

"Exactly. How can I concentrate on this huge undertaking if I'm constantly thinking about what was, what used to be, and what isn't? How can I focus my energy on being a family if I can't be a wife to my husband? I can't let my anger destroy everything I've ever wanted. I can't let my pride ruin my only hope for a secure and stable home life. So I've decided."

{"Decided what, exactly?"}

"Decided that my husband is the father of this baby and I refuse to entertain any thoughts that would destroy that. I've wanted…needed to be a part of something this special and this wonderful all of my life, I can't lose it now."

{"Okay, I get that. But are you *only* staying because of the baby? Do you want your husband at all?"}

As I started to answer, I paused. Speechless, I returned to where I began—on the floor, holding myself, rocking back and forth. Suddenly, a thought occurred to me. I got up and ran to the top dresser drawer where I kept my journal. Returning to my seat on the floor by the toilet, I began to read through the entries that I'd penned during the last few months.

"The answer has got to be in here."

As I read, tears fell onto the pages. A picture was being painted for me. I could no longer deny what was right before my eyes. After reaching the very last entry, I fumbled through my purse for a pen.

{"Writing in your journal has always been therapy for you."}

That was what this entire experience had been for me—therapy. Together, my journal, Manny, and even that insufferable voice guided me through waves of emotions and storms of guilt due to past mistakes. Now here I was staring at a blank page deciding what words I should write, what feelings to express, and what path I would take. That empty page represented a clean slate, a new chance to start over. Whatever I wrote today would determine what my tomorrow would become. After so many reflections, I finally began…*Dear Journal….*

Chapter 32

The Journal—Part Eleven

Dear Journal,

I've been reviewing and researching many major events that occurred in my life in the hopes of pinpointing exactly where I lost myself. Was it when I first saw Manny? Was it when he and I made love for the first time? Was it when I lost him—for good? Or was it when I found out that my husband had been unfaithful? When did I lose the essence of Olivia?

Perhaps all of those milestones shaped me in various ways. It could be said that just meeting Manny altered the future woman I'd become. As soon as I saw him, ***I could only see him****. After he and I were intimate for the very first time that single-minded compulsion developed into a deep-rooted connection. No matter where each of us was in the world, we could sense the other taking a breath. So when I lost Manny after the devastation in Lansing, I truly lost a part of myself. I think that's because Manny made me who I was. He put the stars into my universe. He put the rainbow in my sky. He put love into my heart. When he left, he took all of those things with him. At the very least, however, my universe was still intact. Gradually, I was able to go on and find new stars and new rainbows to illuminate my stratosphere.*

On the other hand, memories of my husband's confession have revealed that he was the one who destroyed my Milky Way. His infidelity left a void as empty and deep as any black hole. So, the irony is Manny created Olivia, and my husband destroyed her.

I believe that's why Manny's return was not only welcomed, but also desperately needed. Somehow our connection always led him back to me, especially when he could make the most difference in my life.

For years, I shut out my feelings of longing for Manny. I made myself happy with my husband. I was committed to our marriage, and no matter how important Manny had been in my past, I was determined to make my husband my future. However, his admission of guilt left me unguarded. The entire experience sent my system into shock—I no longer had the immunity to combat my desire for Manny. I thought my feelings were inconsequential. I hadn't seen or heard from Manny in five long years. I had no idea that my fantasies would find an outlet in the form of his return.

Memories of our love began to overwhelm my senses. As each day passed, Manny was becoming more alive within me. At first, I could picture his face, and then I remembered the way his hair smelled. Soon, I could hear his voice whisper "I love you, Olivia" in my ear. His gentle touch manifested in my dreams. As innocent moments were fondly called to mind, moments of ecstasy and erotic fancy bulldozed their way into my head. It became worse than it had been when I was a teenager having nightmares and seeking closure. Floodgates of unrequited love were opened and drowned out my pain.

As my husband slowly replaced Manny after Lansing, Manny was now conquering the land my husband once called home. I took refuge in memories of Manny. I felt solace while dreaming of Manny. I was at peace thinking of Manny. Manny became the eye of my storm. Maybe his love could heal me, oh how I wished something could.

As a result, his arrival into my life became a double-edged sword. I wanted him there to cut out my sadness, but loving him splintered my soul. When the opportunity presented itself, when Manny appeared before me, I pounced.

Consequently, that moment initiated my descent into a double life.

It's taken so much energy to accept visits from Manny and to go through the motions with my husband. I'm exhausted! But what has been more draining than anything is staying angry all the time. Up until just a few days ago, that anger has rested on my shoulders like a medieval yoke of slavery.

I've come to realize that anger has its place. It can be so satisfying! Especially when it's justified. Then on the other hand, it can be so restrictive and burdensome that it suffocates the life right out of you.

Truly, I've discovered what madness is! I have what I've always wanted, Manny's love and undivided attention. Curiously, though, I can't let go of my husband. I've discovered that with him I have true loyalty. My husband has wanted to stick by me through this difficult time. Then Manny arrives and wants to save me and whisk me away to a forbidden paradise. (Again, the irony is not lost on me.) Manny seemed like he fit the old adage, "When the going gets tough, the tough gets the hell outta' Dodge!" But my husband has what one would call "pesky perseverance"! ***Why can't I have them both?***

Think about! Manny's passionate, romantic, exotic, erotic love compared to my husband's tender, compassionate, loyal, long-suffering love. Putting those ingredients together makes an undeniable, unbelievable, unstoppable man of my dreams!

I can't deny that my husband still means so much to me. Now that Manny has begun to seek more of a commitment from me, I've begun to see the importance of my commitment with my husband. All of a sudden, I'm not angry anymore. Sure, I'm still hurt and still a little wary. But...I'm also still...very much in love with my sweet husband. The one who managed to come running into the house with a busted forehead because something he was working on led to a temper tantrum. Just the thought of his antics gives rise to a chuckle.

But he's also the one who sat by my bedside watching while I slept. The one who took time off work to take care of me when I was sick. The one who brought me roses, just to cheer me up. He makes me smile.

I can no longer deny that I still have a connection with him…I still want to explore what we have…I still ***love*** *my husband…I still* ***want*** *my husband.*

Perhaps Manny has started to sense that. Maybe his proposal or…ultimatum opened my eyes to the fact that ***I can't have Manny and my husband****, I'd have to choose. And although I want him to know how much he means to me, I have chosen to continue loving my husband. Manny needs to know how much our time together has helped me to heal. Without it, I could have never found my way back home. And with a baby on the way… I sincerely want this marriage and this family to be the one that he or she grows up in. I really do want to stay with my husband and make this work. As unexpected as these revelations are…I'm actually happy with this newfound enlightenment!*

Now that I've realized what I have, how am I going to preserve it? I could quietly break things off with Manny and be as I've said before, much worse than my husband ever was. Or I could 'fess up and tell them both the truth about… everything! I could lose everything!

I need to let Manny know how important his presence has meant to me while saying good-bye, all without destroying him or my marriage. On the other hand, Manny might not accept rejection gracefully. He'd always been the one doing the rejecting; I don't know if he'll know how to handle it.

Thinking about confessing my affair to my husband is petrifying. I finally know how he felt, keeping that secret for so long, constantly worrying about losing what we had. I get it now. He made a mistake and he wanted to take it back—but he couldn't. It changed him and ironically made him a better person. I get it now. He risked telling me the truth and losing everything to gain what he'd always wanted. And now I have to do the same. I get it now.

From here on out, history is writing itself. Tonight, I plan to reveal my decision to Manny and unveil my betrayal to my husband. Tonight is the night that I hope for the best and expect the worst. This ends now. I can no longer continue living this double life. Nonetheless, the thought of losing them both and ending up with nothing scares me the most. I do love them both. But I have finally awakened to the fact that I need my husband and all that we mean to each other. ***Finally…I get it now.***

Chapter 33

Saying Goodbye

{"Do you think you're ready for this?"}

I'd better get ready.

Hurriedly, I scampered from the bathroom floor. I rushed to gather up the evidence, throwing the pregnancy test and its packaging into a bag. As I ran to grab my car keys, I threw the bag in the garbage.

That should do it, I thought. *I'd hate for my husband to find out about the baby before I get a chance to tell him everything.*

On the way out the door, I left a message for Manny to meet me at our usual spot. Somehow, I knew he'd arrive right on time.

During the drive, I was surprised by the spectrum of emotion I was feeling. I wasn't looking forward to hurting Manny or my husband. I didn't want to see anguish on either of their faces. However, I was eagerly awaiting the opportunity to end this saga in my life. I didn't know what the future held for my husband and I, but I could finally look toward the future. For the first time, the past had no hold on me.

Taking that journey with Manny through my adolescence, my teenage years and my complex relationship with him, has somehow freed me. I didn't realize until now that I'd been taking everything bad that's ever happened to me *with* me—everywhere! That's no doubt why I started to have trouble making love to my husband, even before I found out about his unfaithfulness. Memories of child molestation, rejection and dejection hovered above me like a storm cloud, constantly raining on my parade. Those memories of lacking love, wanting love and hunting love, all seemed to make it impossible to truly *be* loved. A lost childhood and an unwelcome adulthood tainted each hope and dream.

Suddenly, it was all so clear to me. The problem that led to my affair with Manny wasn't as obvious as I'd previously thought. My motives were much more intricate than revenge or angst. I needed to travel down the same paths that brought me to my husband in the first place. Maybe I always knew, subconsciously, that I'd forgive him for hurting me. So, retracing my steps would help me to find where we went wrong. I thought that all along I was running away from my marriage, when actually, I was *searching* for it.

Manny sat beside me and held my hand while I faced all those demons. He comforted me and reassured me when I wasn't so sure that I could continue on this trip. And now that I'd reached my destination, it was time to say good-bye.

I knew exactly how I felt about Manny; now all I had to do was eloquently find the words to let *him* know. We met at that park at the base of that huge hill. That's where he'd taken me the first night we reconnected. I thought it was only fitting this is where we should let go of one another—forever.

"I got your message," he said as he walked toward me.

"I knew you would," I said, smiling.

He took me by the hand and rocketed me to the top of that mini-mountain. Upon reaching the summit, I could tell that Manny was optimistic. My request to meet him days before the one-week deadline made him confident that the verdict had been reached in his favor.

"Olivia, I knew you'd make the right decision."

"Manny, I have made the right decision, I'm sure of it."

"Well, that sounds good, keep going." His gentle humor made what I had to say even that much more difficult.

"But…."

"Oh, not a '*but*'!" He was still delightfully sweet.

"Well, not, 'but'…rather…." He grabbed my hands and held them in his.

"You always know how to make my fear disappear," I whispered. And then the words I had been searching for began to form on my lips. "Manny, you've been an enormous part of my life for so long. You've helped me to grow. In fact, I've grown up while loving you; I've even grown wiser. Major events in my past have centered around you, so I can never regret knowing or loving you…but…."

"Now there's that 'but' again…." He dropped his head and wouldn't look at me.

"But our time together has passed. The wonderful, whimsical world we shared has evaporated, and whether we like it or not, it's time to return to reality. What we share could never exist here in the real world."

"How can you say that? We're great together!"

"We're great, Manny, when we're tucked away in our cubby hole, but Lansing showed us that the pressures of adulthood and commitment can easily rip us apart."

"I'll just bet this 'reality' you're so anxious to return to—the one that doesn't include me—means your husband and your marriage. Right?" The disappointment rose to the surface.

"Yes, Manny, I'm sorry, but it does. I didn't reach this decision without thoroughly searching my soul. From the moment I laid my eyes on you, you've been apart of me. You've molded me with your love *and* your leaving."

"Why are you harping on that? You know that I always had a good reason for leaving…and I never wanted to leave you. I just had to."

"I'm not trying to accuse you of anything. I do understand why you've had to go away. What I'm saying is you showed me that there was more to me than even I acknowledged. Loving you made me reach for the stars and when you left I thought I couldn't live another day. But somehow I was able to prove to myself that I had the strength and the courage to live and love again. I truly want to thank you for that."

"So…just say it, Olivia. I need to hear you say the words."

"This is goodbye Manny—forever."

Tears began to build in his eyes. "How do you know that you and your husband can make it work? I'm here and I'm not going anywhere this time—because I know how much you need me."

"The truth is I don't know if my husband and I will fully recover from this past year, but I know that I'll be okay from now on. Because you were here when I needed you, I can now return to my life renewed and reborn."

"You're giving up on us and you don't even know if your husband will forgive you."

"I plan to beg his forgiveness and explain everything. The fact is, whether he forgives me or not, I needed to take this journey with you. Now that I have, I know that I'll be just fine. I can finally release myself from past mistakes, rejections and heartbreaks. I can finally breathe without gasping for air." Touching his face gently, I continued, "Manny, you have changed me by allowing me to truly see myself. I'll never forget that and I will always be grateful. If it hadn't been for what we've shared, I couldn't have been helped. I couldn't have been healed."

Gently kissing me as tears ran down his cheeks, *my* Manny whispered, "I told you that I'd always be there when you needed me. I said that I wouldn't let you go unless your husband could give you everything that I can. I need to know for sure that you'll be alright. I have to know that you'll be safe in his hands. I can't leave for good until I know that for sure."

Before I could respond, Manny took off running back down the hill. He moved so fast that it took mere seconds to lose sight of him. I didn't know where he was going or what to expect from him next. I was saddened that complete absolution hadn't been achieved between us, but I knew I had another mission to accomplish.

"Maybe once I can see where things stand with my husband, then I can truly give Manny the closure he's looking for."

After taking a half an hour or so to compose myself and prepare for the confrontation with my husband, I looked down and gently touched my tummy. Then I whispered, "Let's go see your daddy, little one." I headed for home.

As I pulled into the driveway, I noticed that the house was pretty dark inside. Although I was sure my husband was home by then, I was wondering why he was sitting in the house with almost no light. When I walked in, I turned on the lamp by the door. I noticed light shining from our bedroom. So I slowly walked down the hall to reach the glowing doorway.

"Hey, I'm home. Can I talk to you?"

As I turned in the through the opening I caught sight of a historic sight. My husband was standing in our bedroom holding in his hand none other than…my journal. And who was standing beside him? It was none other than…Manny.

My mouth dropped open and my heart pounded erratically. I was speechless.

My husband broke the silence like a bullet through a plate glass window, "*Why…Olivia …**why***?"

Chapter 34

The Longest Night

{"This is going to be the longest night of your life."}

Standing there in awe, trying to absorb the depth of the situation, I knew just how right that damned voice was.

{"How did this happen?"}

At first I couldn't wrap my mind around the situation. As I looked down at my journal, tucked tightly in my husband's hand, a feeling of queasiness flooded my stomach. Then I thought, *Oh my God! I must have left it on the bathroom floor. I was in such a hurry I forgot to hide it. He has to know everything now!*

{"The journal! You're worried about the journal! Do you see Manny over there? Maybe you should be worried about him!"}

Still staring at me, my husband repeated his question, "Why?" By that moment, his voice was trembling as a dam of tears began to burst.

I was so engrossed in the vision of my husband and Manny standing side by side that another few moments passed before I could reply.

{"Your silence is only making this worse. Go ahead, Olivia, end this thing, so you can start over."}

That voice could always be counted on—even when no one else could. Right or wrong, the truth would often ring in my ears.

Before I could say anything, my husband threw the journal on the floor and grabbed the suitcase from under the bed.

"What are you doing?"

"What does it look like?" he said angrily as he started scooping clothes from the dresser drawers.

Manny just stood there silently, watching the events unfold.

"Wait a minute." I rushed over to stop his frantic packing. "Wait a minute, damn it! We need to talk!"

"Talk about what? There's nothing left to talk about!"

"There's a lot to talk about!" I grabbed his arm. "I need to know how much you know."

"I know all I need to know! There's someone else and there's no room for me!"

"You don't understand the whole story."

Uncontrollably upset, he said, "I've been fighting a losing battle for almost a year. You had no intention of forgiving me and giving us another chance! It's over, Olivia."

Those words scared me to death. I started to think that I was too late and that I couldn't fix the damage that was done. Tears streamed down my cheeks as my husband stormed past me and headed for the bedroom door.

"I'll be back for the rest of my stuff in a few days."

Grabbing the suitcase, I watched as he crossed the threshold and stepped into the hallway. I followed my husband into the living room, Manny followed us both, maintaining his silence.

"If you knew everything," I yelled, *"then you'd know that it's you! It's always been you!"*

Still heading out the door, I screamed at my husband, *"You don't understand—give me a chance to make you understand!"*

He didn't respond. He just stopped in his tracks.

"I know this looks bad, but I…I was never unfaithful to you!"

He continued to stand with his back to me.

"Look at me! Please…Manny…look at me!"

He turned to face me.

Staring into ***my husband's*** eyes, I continued. *"Manny, it's always been you!"*

As my words lingered in the air, I watched as Manny, ***my love affair and my fantasy***, smiled while walking slowly toward my husband and then…***faded as they met***.

There was no longer any denying the fact that *Manny and my husband were the same person*—well, different personas—same body.

"What the hell is going on, Olivia?"

"I don't know how to tell you this without sounding like I've lost my mind."

"I think you'd better figure out a way." By then his voice had regained stability. However, mine had not.

"Well, you were right when you said that you've been fighting a losing battle and that I never had any intention of forgiving you."

"What are you telling me?"

"…But you started losing the battle long before that night with that girl. You've been losing me…slowly, for years." As tears rolled down paths along my face, I struggled to continue. *"I never wanted to admit how unhappy I was—not to you—not even to myself."*

My husband interrupted, "Then why should I stay? Sounds to me like you've made up your mind." He turned to walk out the door again.

"There's so much more to this story! Just hear me out—please!"

After dropping the suitcase, and closing the door, my husband seated himself on the couch and then silently waited for me to continue. I also sat down and tried to summon all of my strength. I knew I was going to need just that to get through this night.

Calmly, I began again. "From the moment I first saw you, there has been no one else for me. I can't remember a time, since I became aware that you existed, that I've thought about or desired any other man. You were 'it' for me; there's never been anyone else. I heard a funny thing the other day on some TV show. Some guy said that no matter how happy you are in a relationship with someone, you'll always wonder about the one that got away. They'll always be some small doubt as to whether that person, the one who slipped through your fingers, was 'the one.' I chuckled when I heard that because I knew that for me that just was not the case. 'The one' for me didn't get away at all—I married him," I said with a smile.

My husband's face softened, slightly, but I knew there was much more work to be done.

"When we first met there was an inferno that burned between us. There was passion in our kiss, there was electricity in our touch, and there was a blaze in our bed. You blew into my life like some powerful windstorm that swept me away. You changed me, Manny, you changed the way I looked at the world."

Searching my eyes, he asked, "How did I do that?"

"You were a girl's fantasy and then some! You were sexy, confident and thrilling. I'd never known that a man like you could exist outside of a soap opera or a romance novel. And I never thought a man like you would ever fall in love with a girl like me." I dropped my head, intentionally eluding his stare.

"I asked myself, often, what a guy like you saw in me. You were physically chiseled and beautifully sculpted. You were artistically talented and sexually gifted. What was I? Just a shy, quiet bookworm living in a bubble of college entrance exams and soap opera fantasies. What did I have to offer you? But I was just so overwhelmed with your love and your presence in my life, I refused to allow myself to ruin it by forcing the issue. And then something changed in me."

"What?"

"The more I spent time with you, the more I wanted you. Eventually, I found myself wanting you so much that I could barely think of anything else and then…you were gone."

"That was a lifetime ago, Olivia."

"Not really. The very first time that I had to deal with you walking out on me was after I broke Josh's heart to be with you. You remember that don't you?"

"Oh, yeah," he said with a grin. "I remember you dumped that guy for me."

"So you must also remember how you dumped me, shortly thereafter."

"You know why I had to break your heart—because of my parents. We've been through this, I didn't want to do it, but I thought it would make my life easier to just forget about you. My mom and dad were not going to let me date a black girl."

"But you didn't forget about me, did you? You didn't let me go. You just came back for me—whenever convenient for you and impossible for me."

"What was impossible? So, you were dating some other guy, but you didn't love him, you loved me."

"Yes, that's true, but he didn't know that. Poor Malcolm had no clue who he was up against. I didn't either. I didn't realize until later, just how powerful your hold on me really was."

"Not too powerful because you don't feel those things about me anymore."

"I'm getting there. I'll admit that the first time I broke up with Malcolm it had a lot to do with how crappy he was as a boyfriend. But I probably would have put up with him, if it weren't for you." I looked over at him and smiled. "If it weren't for you, Manny, my life would have been so different."

"Apparently, it would have been better."

"I never said that. Actually, it would have been much more boring." We both chuckled at that comment.

"Truthfully though, all of this talk of the past is leading me somewhere. Now, when you left again, and Malcolm and I started dating again, I honestly thought I'd never see you again. I tried so hard to forget about you, but you know how that went."

"I tried to forget about you too. I knew I had only caused you pain and I had every intention of leaving you alone to be happy."

"But you didn't. Again, you came for me."

"I couldn't stay away. You were the only woman who'd ever loved me—unconditionally. I needed that. I needed you."

"I needed you too. I knew from the moment you contacted me again that I wouldn't be able to stay with Malcolm. The desire to be with you pulled me in your direction constantly. Whether I liked it or not, I couldn't fight what we had."

"So…where did that go?"

"Well…I think it walked out the door with you in Lansing."

I obviously struck a nerve; my husband then avoided my glare. "I hated leaving you there. But after everything…I didn't have a choice."

"Yes, I know. After everything...everything that we still don't talk about. Everything...."

"You know what that place did to me...what it did to us!"

"Yeah. I know that all of our dreams fell apart when I moved there. We were desperate to be together, so you quit your job and moved there prematurely. You didn't have another job lined up and we barely had enough money to find an apartment. Things started off pretty badly."

"I wish you'd never gone there. Things could have been so different...I'd be different. I'd be the person you first fell in love with, if you'd never moved away from me."

"I thought about that too. See, I told you that I was getting somewhere by talking about the past and now I think I just got there."

"What do you mean?"

"Manny, for the passed three months I've been living a fantasy with the man I first met when I was a fifteen-year-old girl. I've been talking to, confiding in and making love with...an illusion."

"That sounds...well...like...like...."

"Like I should be locked up in a padded room."

"Well, I didn't want to say that, but...yeah." He smiled.

"I know how it sounds. But this experience has truly felt real to me. And I'm so glad that I've been through it."

"Why?"

"Because, for some reason, I didn't have the courage to examine my life, my marriage and myself—alone. I needed someone there to guide and comfort me. And since there has never been anyone in my life that I've loved or trusted more than you, it made sense that my guide on this spiritual journey be... *you*."

"So let me get this straight. There was never any man—any *real* man that you fell in love with or had sex with. This whole time you've been *pretending*."

"I guess you could call it that, but it was so much more. After I found out about you and that girl, I...I just got lost. Things were already not the way I'd envisioned they would be for us, mostly because of the catastrophe in Lansing, but finding out that you were unfaithful sent me spiraling out of control. At first, I was just trying to fight the pain and the anger. I wanted to have the strength to finally leave you and be done with it."

"Thanks," he interjected sarcastically.

"But then I started going over my life from as far back as I could remember. I was in so much pain over you that I think my defense mechanism kicked in. I wanted to leave you, but that pull, the one that I thought was diminishing, kept me here with you."

"So when did *I* first appear?"

"That night when you asked me why I was staying with you if I was so unhappy. Remember, I ran out the door and drove away. I didn't come back until late that night."

"Yeah, I do remember that."

"That night, I envisioned seeing you at jazz club by mere chance. But then you and I ran off to that hill, the one at the park."

"The hill that we used to go to talk when we first got back from Lansing?"

"That's the one. That night I laid on the top of that hill and played out in my head what it would be like to have you—the old you—appear and take my fears and pain away." I dropped my head as tears resurfaced. *"It felt so good to feel you again. It felt wonderful to be the way we were when you lived on Hoover. It felt so good to escape reality. I didn't realize it, but soon I was escaping to this place with you more and more. Eventually, it was as if I became addicted to the safety and predictability of my fantasy world. I shut you out to hide there with…the old you. I'm so ashamed, Manny. I'm so ashamed."*

Manny, my sweet husband, walked over to where I was sitting and held me tightly. "There's nothing to be ashamed of. We've both shut each other out during these passed few years and we've both changed. Think about it. When we moved in together after you came back from school, we didn't even talk about what we'd been through. We sort of just pretended like nothing happened and we tried to start from that moment."

"I remember that. It was like I decided to put the entire drama behind me and not even look at you as the person I'd met and loved

before that time."

"In a way, you were right to feel that way because I wasn't the same person. I even cut my hair, and gradually I stopped working out as much and even gained a few pounds."

Hearing my husband admit those things about himself made me feel admiration for him.

My voice lost its quiver. "I don't blame you for changing, especially on the outside. You cut your hair because you were desperate to find work and you thought if you had a clean-cut look you'd be more acceptable to employers."

"It didn't yield the results I wanted right away, but eventually I found a good job."

"And I don't want you to feel bad about your physique. We all put on weight as we grow older, but you had other obstacles to overcome."

"If you can call having my entire weight set and bench stolen an obstacle."

"Well, you worked out religiously before all the chaos started. Moving from place to place, looking for work, trying to visit me at MSU and losing parts of yourself along the way—all of those things were obstacles. Lifting weights and exercising had to take a back seat to the problems you were dealing with. I never thought less of you for that."

"If you weren't blaming me for that, then what were you blaming me for?"

That was a good question. I suppose I was blaming my husband for everything else that had gone wrong. I certainly wasn't accepting responsibility for any part I played in our life's disastrous course. The reality of it was: I wasn't being fair to a man who lost everything for loving me.

Again, I began to weep; I could hardly speak. Through tears of utter shame, I said, *"I can't deny it anymore. It's my fault. I'm the real reason why you ended up with that girl."*

"What are you talking about?"

"I did this to you! I did this to us! *I've been keeping you at arm's* *length for years. At first, it was because I couldn't face the reality about our trials and our failures. And then it was because I didn't want to admit that when you needed me, I deserted you. I didn't want to accept the person you had become and I couldn't face the reasons why you were changing. Without really knowing it, I was pushing you away, pushing you out of my heart. So, you sought refuge in some sexual favor that you regretted, confessed and apologized for, but I'm the one who should be apologizing. I've hurt* ***you*** *so much."*

Hearing me apologize shook my husband. He couldn't respond right away. A brief silence allowed time for me to compose myself. Slowly my interest in Manny's sympathy waned; *I began to think only of regaining his love*. I needed to make him understand that I still wanted what ***he*** had to offer.

The more I unloaded my pain, the stronger I became. I was able to stop crying and continue. "These passed few months, when I chronicled ***'my affair'*** with, well…you…I was doing something that I'd never attempted before. I was, pretty much, moving within a virtual reality, one that consisted of illusions and memories, trying to make sense of myself. That's why I couldn't open up about my feelings. I couldn't reveal things in a way that you could understand when I didn't understand them myself."

"So, you starting writing them down."

The tension was slowing seeping out of the room.

"Exactly. Writing down all of my greatest moments and my biggest tragedies gave me the perspective I needed. You were right when you picked up on my indifference. I just wasn't aware of it at the time. When the opportunity arrived to look at you as a person and not just as a fantasy man that I eyed while riding my bike down a street less traveled, I didn't rise to the occasion. Long before that infamous night with that girl, ***I failed*** *you*."

"Listen Olivia, I'm not trying to blame you for what I did. I told you before, no matter what's going on between us, I'm not owed an orgasm—or anything else for that matter! You didn't force me to drop my pants that night. I was the idiot—not you."

"I know you're not trying to blame me. And that's the problem.

I've been blaming ***you*** for everything! I've been punishing you for letting me down and not just that night. Subconsciously, I've been trying to keep my distance while going through the motions of marriage."

My husband surprisingly understood. "I think we've both been doing that. Not only have we been going through the motions, but we've also been sweeping things under the rug and avoiding our real feelings."

I couldn't believe how insightful and compassionate he was, I'd overlooked those qualities for far too long. "That's true, Manny, I know that we've both been less than forthcoming with our deepest thoughts and feelings."

"Since you agree with me, then answer this question and be honest: Where do we go from here?"

Before I could respond, he continued, "You've obviously missed what we had. You missed the guy you saw standing in front of his house with his martial arts muscle and unwavering confidence. You missed our hot, intense sex and our deep connection. From where I'm sitting, it looks like you've settled for what we have now. You just settled for me. There's not much left of the old me to dream about. It seems like I've lost everything that made me…me."

Manny couldn't look at me after those words. He had lost his family, his job, his apartment, his best friend, and most devastating, his belief in himself. Unbelievably, I didn't find out until this night just how close I came to losing Manny forever. As if all of that weren't enough, when he came back from Lansing three weeks after retrieving his beloved Helix from a friend who'd been nice enough to store it for him, some moron pulled out in front of him, causing the Helix to broadside the car, leaving the motorcycle a mangled mess. So, Manny ended up losing that too. Although, he was thrown off the bike into oncoming traffic and almost killed, his helmet and the quick thinking of the driver in the other lane saved his life. Slamming on their brakes, they narrowly avoided crushing his skull. Miraculously, the entire ordeal left him with only one cracked rib, a few bruises and several abrasions.

Shocked and trembling, I asked, "You've kept this secret for years. You said that your bike was stolen. You never told me that you were in an accident!"

"How could I tell you? I didn't want to think about how I almost died. It was easier to just say the bike had been stolen. You accepted that story and I didn't have to talk about it anymore."

Dropping his head, my husband whispered, "I was being stripped naked. I felt like a failure and I couldn't imagine why you would want to stay with me after seeing me exposed and helpless like that."

"But I did stay."

"I know. Unfortunately…you changed."

I conceded, "At the time, I didn't see it. I realize it now though."

"The fact that you stuck it out through some really hard times helped me to believe that you still loved me, but the look in your eyes contradicted that conclusion. I wasn't sure what you saw in me anymore. All I knew was, I didn't see anything in myself. I wondered everyday when you would leave."

"You never mentioned that."

"I didn't want you to leave. I thought if I brought it up, it would…well…put it out there and make you think it was okay. I didn't want to lose you. With each day that passed, you stayed and I was happy just for that."

"So even though I was making you feel so horrible, you were still glad that we were together?"

"On your worst day, you loved me more than any other woman I'd known on their best day. I needed you. I accepted whatever you were willing to give."

And he did. Throughout those months when we were trying to forget about our mistakes in Lansing and focus on a future together, I became increasing distant, especially sexually. Manny accepted whatever he got from me…until that one night at least. I suppose the rejection began to weigh heavy on him, he could no longer bear it.

"I can't tell you how much I've longed to reach out to you, Manny. You were—and still are—handsome and sexy! I was just being selfish. It was like I was imprisoned inside myself. On the inside, I felt love and desire for you. But outwardly, I was cold and unwelcoming. I just wanted time to stand still for us. I didn't want you to change. I wanted to hide and be safe in the past, like that summer we spent on Hoover. I just wanted that again. The fact that you were unemployed a lot, cut your hair, and lost your fire, all made me realize that we couldn't hide from reality. Damn it! No matter what we did or how hard we tried, we couldn't hide and we couldn't stop growing up and growing older." I dropped my head and whispered, "I was being selfish. For so long, I've been selfish. I haven't tried to see your point of view at all. Why in the world do you still want to be with me?"

Manny lifted my head with his hand, "There's a lot of reasons, but one that must be said above all else is you just couldn't do it."

"I couldn't do what?"

"For starters, you couldn't leave me. No matter how bad you were feeling about our situation, and me, you stayed everyday. And when you found out about what I did, you could have left, or kicked me out, but you didn't—you stayed. You stayed with me, when no else would."

"I couldn't leave you…I just couldn't…."

"I know. And even when you wanted to look for comfort with somebody else, you didn't allow the fact that I'd been unfaithful give you the green light to do the same. You obviously loved me so much that you would rather *imagine* making love to the old me than let some stranger touch you. I wish I had been even half as strong and long suffering as you've been. Maybe then, I wouldn't have screwed up so badly."

"Manny, please don't."

"Don't what?"

"You're making me out to be some innocent victim through all of this and I'm far from it. I've been torturing you these passed five years. I…I'm not what you think I am."

"Why are you being so hard on yourself?"

"Because even though I wanted to let you in, I didn't. Maybe I was just looking for excuses to shut you out."

"I know there were other things…like…car problems, credit card bills, medical bills, back taxes, parking tickets, and the infamous…Bonneville."

That list of unfortunate, but stressful elements of life was pretty typical of most married couples. However, that car, that Bonneville was one of the biggest backbreaking straws to ever meet a camel!

"Yeah, that Bonneville…I mean *Lady Bonneville*. The old girl sure was one of ***those things*** that added gallons of water to the moat around my fortress!"

I was trying to keep things light at that point. But the truth was still very painful.

"Olivia, don't try to hide it. I know how much you hate that car."

"No, just you for bringing it here," I whispered, but still audible.

"Oh, I know. You've told me. Then again, you could never really hate me, could you?"

My husband's tone of voice was reminiscent of the Manny I'd known so long ago. I saw a little glimmer in his eye as he flashed a smile.

"No, I guess, I really couldn't hate you…no matter how hard I tried." I found myself being coy and blushing at the thought.

"Olivia, please tell me…tell me what that car did to make you so upset."

"Manny, you know it's not the car itself. It's what it represents. That car came into our lives when you promised to put all of your energy toward restoring our marriage. Instead, you spent nearly every free moment trying to restore that piece of crap in the driveway!"

"Hush now," he said mockingly, "she might hear you."

At first I was not amused. My mouth dropped open as I jumped from my seat. "I'm leaving."

"Oh, no!" Manny said as he grabbed me and spun me in his arms. When I was facing him, he said, "You're not leaving yet; you're going to miss the best part."

I couldn't help but smile. "The best part of what?"

"The best part of our **new life** together."

Gently, he guided me to the bedroom where we both took a seat on the bed.

"What's that supposed to mean?"

"I mean that I'm tired of this old garbage. I'm tired of the past and I'm tired of the storm cloud that's been hovering over us for half a decade! I'm tired of not being as happy as I want to be with you. Hell, I'm just tired!"

Again, I couldn't fight the smile that attacked my face.

"I want to start over. I just need to know one thing."

I was curious as to where my husband was going, but I had a feeling that I'd like where we'd end up. "What's that?"

"I need to know what stopped it?"

"What stopped what?"

"What stopped your…fantasy life? What stopped the old me from taking you away?"

"It's funny you should ask that."

"Why?"

"Because, the answer is kind of weird." He looked at me and snickered. I continued, "When I realized the end of my spiritual journey was near, 'Manny' did something that shocked my senses."

Smiling, he asked, "What did he do?"

"He asked me to leave you and marry him."

"What? How can that be?"

"I think it was just my way of snapping out of it. I knew I could never have that person again. I needed some way to reconcile all of my feelings about the past and the old you. When 'Manny' proposed marriage, it just reaffirmed the fact that my fantasy man could never live outside of a fantasy."

"Yeah, but I used to be real."

"I know, sweetheart, but…but truthfully, the old Manny couldn't survive in the real world anymore than my illusion of him could."

"Why is that?"

"Because that young guy had to grow up and deal with life. That guy had to turn into a man and leave the fantasy world behind. When I turned the 'you' down, I symbolically accepted that. I realized that what we had, as beautiful and special as it was, doesn't compare to the commitment and the bond that we've developed in marriage. This marriage…you…are all I want, now and always."

"I finally know for sure, that no matter how hard things get between us, you'll love me…only me."

"Well that's great for you! But now what?" I was slightly irreverent.

"Now, oh, now I get rid of that Bonneville."

When I heard those words, I was glad I had already been sitting.

"What?"

"Consider her outta here! I'll put an ad in the Auto Trader, the Classifieds, the Online Marketplace—anywhere to sell it and get it out of the driveway and out of our lives."

"But you love that car, Manny, why would you do that?"

"Because I love you more than that car or anything else in the world! I wasn't kidding. We're starting over. From this moment, we're going to make 'Manny and Olivia' mean something new. We're not going to carry our mistakes around like sandwich boards on our backs anymore. We're not going to allow ourselves to be marked with some scarlet letter for making bad decisions. I think we've suffered enough, don't you?"

I was floored. "Yes. I was thinking exactly the same thing! I told you that I came to tell you everything tonight. I wanted to move on, toward a future together, without looking back. It's like a weight that I've had strapped to my shoulders has suddenly turned into a feather. Nothing else matters to me—not Lansing, not the past, not that car, and not that one night. Manny…I forgive you. Finally after all of this time, I've allowed myself to see things through your eyes. You didn't deserve my apathy and I don't want to punish you one more second."

As I spoke, Manny's hands caressed mine. I could see a change right before my eyes.

"Olivia, I've never known love, before I met you. I've never felt it, I've never touched it, and I've never tasted it, before you. Despite our problems, I've known true love, because you've given it to me. And I promise that from now on we're going to *share* in that love.

No more secrets, no more tension, no more loneliness, no more pain. Olivia, we're in this *together*."

His words were so tender and genuine. I felt my heart pound dramatically. For the first time in years, Manny and I were at the same place, understanding and forgiving each other.

Cautiously, he leaned over to kiss me. As his tender lips touched mine, I felt a relief that I deeply missed. Slowly, his tongue sought out its mate. In time, my husband and I were entangled in the most passionate kiss we'd shared since before we were married. And then it happened. A tidal wave of emotion caused a gush within my loins. The intensity of the moment was overpowering. I could tell Manny sensed it too. Seconds into the surge, he began removing my blouse. Before I realized it, I was being picked up and gently laid on my back. Somehow, the old Manny had returned to me through my husband's new view on life. I say that because as things heated up, he pulled back to take his time with me. As excited as we both were, after laying me in a comfortable position, he ever so slowly finished undressing me. By the time he was done, the bed was soaked beneath me.

In true Manny form, he stayed dressed as he worked, caressing and kissing every inch of my body. He loved to see my nakedness stretched out before him as he stood over me. It was like I was being offered to him on an altar. He loved to show his powerful restraint by slowly and meticulously scrutinizing every inch of me, rather than hungrily and hurriedly pouncing.

"Don't worry, Olivia," he whispered. "You're finally going to have the best of both of us."

{"Damn, girl, you've got it made now!"}

I secretly smirked at that voice's raunchy humor.

Hearing his voice during this erotic moment sent me swirling through time and space. Not only did it remind me of the good ol' days, but it also revealed what I had to look forward to in the future. All of those thoughts distracted me, momentarily from my husband's quick undressing. I opened my eyes to see him standing nude before me. The space underneath me was drenched. Instead of merely positioning himself on top of me, Manny softly lay beside me. Smiling, he whispered, “This is going to be the longest night of your life.”

And truly, it was!

Chapter 35

The Beginning

The next morning when I awoke, I felt as if I had been reborn. Lying nude in my husband's arms was exhilarating. In fact, I couldn't remember ever feeling that invigorated, enthusiastic or optimistic. As I listened to my husband breathe softly beside me, I could see the image of our new life beckoning to me. Finally free from the burdens of anguish, guilt and disappointment, I felt myself practically floating between the sheets. For countless moments, I stared into space, daydreaming, planning and anticipating.

"There is so much to be done," I gleefully whispered to myself. "There are so many plans to be made. I have waited so long to be liberated that I can hardly keep all of these thoughts and emotions under control. I feel like I'm going to burst!"

{"Well, make sure when you explode, you let the truth splatter all over Manny."}

"The truth? I've told him the truth."

"I know you've told him the truth, but aren't you forgetting something? Or should I say someone."}

Smiling profusely, I giggled in response. "I haven't forgotten him…or her," I said as I touched my belly. "I'm just waiting for the right time to tell Manny. Last night was already so overwhelming that I didn't want this news to be overshadowed by the work that needed to be done."

{"So when is the right time?"}

Before I could contemplate the answer, my husband's touch jarred my concentration.

As he kissed my shoulder he quietly spoke, "I love you, Olivia."

"I love you too…Manny."

We held each other for what seemed like eons, silently peering into each other's thoughts. I had not felt that in tune with my husband in years. I wanted to blurt out the news of my pregnancy, but the gentle moment we were sharing was so tranquil, I didn't want it to come to an end. By the time I decided to reveal my gift, my husband was leaving our bed.

"Sorry, Hun, but I've got to get going."

"What? Where are you going? It's Saturday!" The disappointment dripped from my voice.

"Don't worry, I'm just on a mission. I'll be back soon."

In a flash he was out the door. Despite my husband's quick departure, my elation was unaffected. Last night had changed so much for me. I trusted Manny and myself. I was sure of our solidity and of our love.

{"So when are you going to tell him the good news?"}

That voice re-entered my thoughts.

"I've been thinking about this for hours; I really don't know when I should tell him."

{"Why?"}

"Because this is only the beginning. Manny and I have only just begun to reconnect and share in each other. What if he's not ready for a baby?"

{"Well, it's a little too late for that. But, what are you afraid of?"}

"I'm not afraid…really. I'm more cautious than afraid."

{"What is there to be cautious about?"}

"So many things. I truly believe that Manny has made a renewed commitment to me, but what if the news of this baby makes him feel obligated? What if Manny starts to feel overwhelmed and unsure about fatherhood?"

{"What if…? What if Manny is over the top, scream it from the mountains excited to find out that he's going to be a dad with the woman he loves more than anything? I thought you trusted your love. What happened to that?"}

"I do trust our love, I just want to give it time to…oh, who am I kidding? The truth is, once I tell someone, it then becomes more than just two blue lines on a plastic stick. Maybe I'm not as ready as I thought I was."

{"Don't worry, Olivia. There is no one else more ready to be a mama than you."}

"How can you say that?"

{"You've believed deeply in family all of your life. You were just one of the unfortunates who didn't grow up in a well-adjusted home with two parents who were in love and bonded by their wedding vows."}

"I know. I definitely wouldn't want my children growing up the way that I did."

{"That's exactly what I mean. You have already made an internal choice to give your children a better life, a happy life. Now that you and your husband have found each other again, there's no reason why this little baby can't grow up in a warm, loving and united family. You can give him or her the childhood you always wanted, but could never have."}

While taking the time to bathe and dress, I contemplated that voice's argument. Though, my train of thought was briefly interrupted by a fit of nausea; morning sickness still had a hold on me. After which, I was able to conclude that I was more ready to be a mother than I realized. A family is what I've always wanted and I was determined to do everything right.

"The last few months has enlightened me fully to my strengths and weaknesses. I've tapped my inner well of sadness and gloom until it dried out. I've searched the boundaries of my soul and reached down to the roots of my very being. I can't say that there won't be any further adversity or tragedy, but I can say that I've discovered something very important."

{"What's that?"}

"I've discovered that I'm up for the challenge. I no longer feel like a victim or an insignificant in my own life. I've finally realized that there is more to me than grieving over my loss of innocence and mourning over years of disappointment. And if there's more to me than meets the eye, then it's possible that I could be a deep ocean of wonders."

{"For once, we agree on something."}

I smiled at the compliment. And then I heard the front door unlock.

"Babe?"

"Manny!" I ran to greet him. "Where have you been? You've been gone for quite a while."

"Well...."

"Well...what?"

"I've been out arranging a surprise for you...actually two surprises."

"Oooh!" I squealed with delight. Jumping up and down, I said, "I wanna see! Gimme!"

My toddler routine made Manny laugh out loud. "Get your shoes on, we're going out in the back yard."

Hurriedly, I complied.

"Close your eyes," Manny said as he led me out the back door. "Now open them."

Excitedly, I popped open my eyes to see revealed in front of me...Lady Bonneville. I couldn't hide my displeasure.

"Oh, Manny, you're kidding right? You've just been teasing me! You know that this car is no surprise for me."

"Olivia, if you stop pouting for a second you can get your surprise. Take a look in the front window."

Staring right at me was a huge 'FOR SALE' sign. "That sign...you put that in the window like you promised."

"It gets better than that."

"What do you mean?"

"There's been a guy at my job who's been hounding me about this car for weeks. He's wanted to buy it from me and finish the restoration job himself. I didn't want to part it with it at the time of his offer, but...now...."

"Now what?"

"Now...today is a new day. I took a chance and went to see that guy. I told him that if he still wanted to make me an offer, the Bonneville was his."

"Well...what did he offer you?"

"He offered me a grand—I accepted."

My chin hit the ground. "He offered you a grand? You mean a thousand dollars?"

"Yep. And I took it. He's coming by this evening with the money. Lady Bonneville will be out of here by the end of the night."

I was overwhelmed by the gesture. Joyfully, I said, "You meant everything you said last night."

"Of course, I did, Honey. I told you that I wanted to start a new life with you and I'm going to do everything in my power to make that happen."

I jumped into my husband's arms and kissed him ravenously.

Moments of sweet kisses were exchanged before he interrupted, "Don't you want your other surprise?"

I'd forgotten about the other surprise. "Yes, of course! But what could top this?"

"Look in the front seat."

I ran over to the passenger door as my husband ran to the driver's side. We both jumped into the seat. I looked down to find a gift-wrapped box beside me.

"Go ahead and open it."

Giddily, I snatched it up and began to rip it open. Inside, I found...a book. I turned it over to find my name engraved in its leather cover. I opened it up and all I found were...blank lined pages.

"What's this sweetie?"

"It's your ***new*** journal—to write about your ***new life***."

"Manny? You bought me a new journal?"

"Yes, because I don't want you to write in the old one anymore. I know how much you love writing and how...um...therapeutic it was to write in the last one. So, I wanted you to keep doing that, but with this new book...you're going to be able to write about our new life, our new love and our new adventures." He grinned intensely.

"I love it! Manny, a gift like this shows just how much you know me. Doing all of this proves how determined you are to keep your promises and to take our marriage in a new direction."

"You did believe me when I told you that I wanted to leave the past far behind us and to look toward the future, didn't you?"

"Of course, but I didn't know you'd move this fast!"

"Now we've got to start making plans for the ceremony."

"The ceremony, what ceremony?"

"The ceremony where we renew our vows, of course."

"You've been thinking about that?"

"Ever since I opened my eyes this morning and saw you lying there in bed, I've been thinking about it. Renewing our vows is exactly what we need to tell the world that we are in a new and wonderful place. Don't you still want to do that?"

Smiling, I slid closer to him and while touching his face, I said softly, "More than anything." After kissing his cheeks, I whispered, "But finding a dress might be sort of difficult."

"Why? I know you're picky, but I'm sure you're find something."

"Finding my size is going to be a challenge."

"Your size? You don't need a muu-muu. What's the problem?"

"In a few months, it **will** be more difficult to find my size. I'm sure to have gained more weight by then." Looking into his eyes, I searched for the moment of comprehension.

"How do you know you're going to put on weight? You're not going to start pigging out are you?"

I didn't respond. I just laughed and looked at him again.

"What? The only way you'd know that you were going to gain weight was if you were…preg—" The moment of comprehension. "You're…. we're…?"

"Manny, my darling, we're going to have a baby!"

"Olivia! When did you find out? How pregnant are you? Have you been to the doctor? How are you feeling? Are you—?"

"Hold on! One question at a time! I found out yesterday, before you and I had a chance to talk. I'm probably only a few weeks along. I haven't been to the doctor yet. And I'm feeling happier than I've ever felt!"

Holding me tightly, he whispered, "Why didn't you tell me yesterday?"

"I just wanted to find the right time."

"It doesn't matter when you told me; all that matters is that I'm going to be a dad! I'm going to have a baby with you, the person I love more than anyone in the world."

We kissed deeply and embraced tightly.

"I'd better get you inside so you can rest."

"Wait, Manny. Don't you want to say good bye to the 'Lady'?"

"Believe it or not Olivia, after everything that's happened in the last 24 hours, I can't even see her. All that matters to me is you."

The rest of the evening was spent quietly puttering around the house. As planned, my husband's co-worker arrived to pick up the Bonneville and paid in full. He drove it out of the driveway and out of our lives. My husband took it quite well. He seemed virtually unaffected, especially since he was very preoccupied with wedding and baby plans. We talked for hours about the future and wrote down several details concerning the upcoming events. That cloud of misery that used to linger above our home was distinctively replaced with a ray of sunshine and hope.

That night, I opened my engraved book. Smiling and with great satisfaction, I penned the words,

> *Dear Journal*
> ***The beginning is at hand….***

* * * * *